GHOST IN THE SHELL 2

INNOCENCE

AFTER THE LONG GOODBYE

GHOST IN THE SHELL 2

INNOCENCE

AFTER THE LONG GOODBYE

MASAKI YAMADA

TRANSLATED BY YUJI ONIKI
WITH CARL GUSTAV HORN

VIZ MEDIA | SAN FRANCISCO

Original animation "Ghost in the Shell 2: Innocence"
© 2004 Shirow Masamune/KODANSHA•IG, ITNDDTD
Text copyright © 2004 Masaki Yamada.
First published in 2004 in Japan by Tokuma Shoten
Publishing Co. Ltd. Original Japanese edition © 2004
TOKUMA SHOTEN PUBLISHING Co., Ltd.
All Rights Reserved.

English translation © VIZ Media, LLC

Illustrations by Daigo Shinma, Keita Saeki
Cover design by Amy Martin

Published by
VIZ Media, LLC
295 Bay St.
San Francisco, CA 94133
www.viz.com

Library of Congress Cataloging-in-Publication Data

Yamada, Masaki, 1950-
 [Inosensu. English]
 Ghost in the shell 2 : innocence : after the long goodbye / by Masaki Yamada ; [English
translation, VIZ Media].
    p. cm.
 "First published in 2004 in Japan by Tokuma Shoten ... "--T.p. verso.
 ISBN-13: 978-1-4215-1394-2 (pbk. : alk. paper)
 ISBN-10: 1-4215-1394-3 (pbk. : alk. paper)
 I. VIZ Media. II. Title. III. Title: Innocence.
 PL865.A497I66 2007
 895.6'35--dc22

                              2007008862

Printed in the U.S.A.
First paperback edition, July 2007

イノセンス
After The Long Goodbye

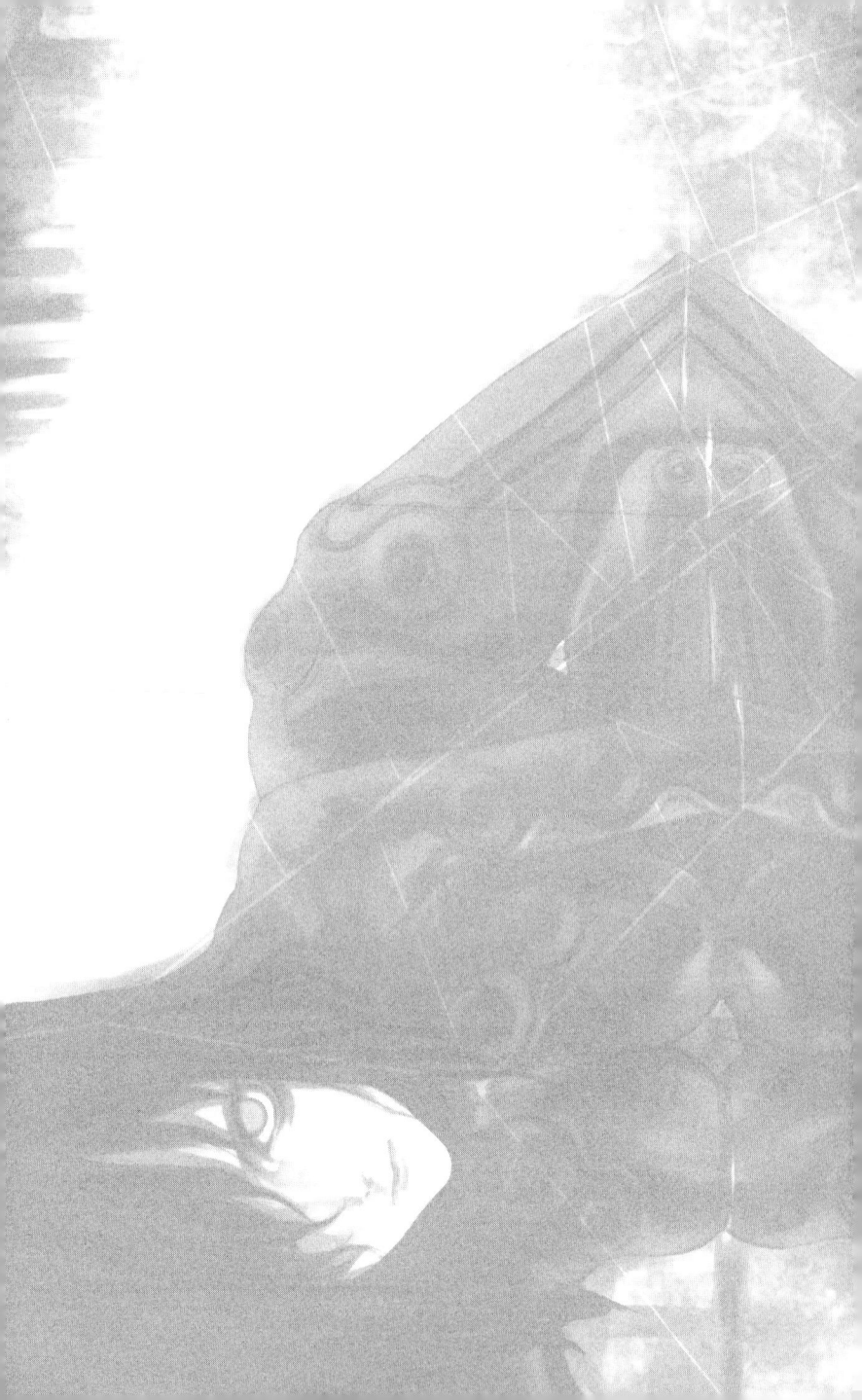

CONTENTS

PROLOGUE

All I have is my dog Gabriel. I have no friends, no lover. My former partner the Major is gone. I have no family. And I don't dream.

And yet, I had a son in my dream.

I loved this dream son, though he vanished when I awoke. I loved him as much as I loved the Major—as I love Gabriel.

My dream son looked five or six years old. He spoke as a child. But when he spoke he talked of things adults couldn't see. He was like Gabu—I call Gabriel that. I thought that if Gabu could speak, she'd talk of those things, too.

I'd look down at my dream son to make sure he wasn't Gabu. Every time I did he would squeeze my hand tight. I loved him so much in my dream.

We were riding the elevator together. My son wanted to press the button for our floor. I had to lift him up because he was too short. He giggled at that. His hair had the dry scent of summer, of hay soaked in the sun. I don't know how I knew that's what it was. I just couldn't seem to recall.

The elevator didn't rise; it descended to the sound of a muted trumpet, stoic and restrained, and mournful beyond belief. Lee Morgan's "I'm a Fool to Want You," I think it was. It played the entire ride down. Most of the time I ignore the tune, until I realize it's always in the back of my mind.

It was like something, that's what I thought. But I had no idea what it was like. There was no reason to dwell on it.

My dream son said, "Dad?"

"Yes?"

"Is it bad to love someone?"

I looked at my son. He looked at me. So our eyes met for a moment. I was the one who looked away.

"What makes you say that? What could be wrong with loving someone?"

"Then, why...," my son stammered. He was on the verge of crying, but ashamed, he held back.

"Why are they going to put —— to sleep?"

I spoke the dog's name, but I couldn't hear what I said. I don't think the name was Gabu. It felt odd to hear another name for a dog.

"Yes."

"—— became too fond of you. His e-brain was over-customized. They mass-produce them. If it's too customized, then you can't re-initialize it anymore. So once the dog's brain expires, they have to dispose of it. That's just the way it works."

"But that doesn't mean it can't *love* someone."

"That's a different matter." I shook my head. "An entirely different matter."

In the dream my son nodded silently. He didn't look at all convinced. He looked desperate, lost, though he was with me. I was worried. I had to do something.

I turned to him again and said, "Will you promise me one thing?"

"Yes."

"They have to put —— to sleep because that's what the law says. But whether you're allowed to love someone or not has no theoretical relevance to that law." Theoretical relevance.

"Okay."

"Of course there's nothing wrong about loving someone. That's what I believe. People have to love each other. That's how they survive. Do you understand?"

"Yes."

"You mustn't confuse that with the fact the dog has to be put to sleep. That's different. I need you to understand that. Will you promise me you understand that?"

"Yes."

"You understand that?"

"I understand."

"You *promise?*"

"I promise."

"Good." I tapped the back of his hand a few times. "You're a good kid."

My son was understanding. He was very considerate of these things. I was proud of him. I was very proud of my son.

We gazed up at the elevator and saw it change its state from floor to floor. The pet termination center was in the lobby. My son and I were going to say goodbye to ours.

And if we wanted the same puppy, we could have requested them to leave a fragment of bone or bit of hair behind. But five or six these days is already old enough to know better. The clone won't repeat the feelings—it only preserves the image of the loss. It had taken many such clones for people to realize.

The elevator passed the second floor; the ground was where they gave the dogs their poison. In a few more moments we would say goodbye. My son squeezed my hand again, wanting to talk.

"Dad."

"What is it?"

I looked into his eyes now for the last time. They were full of tears but still he didn't let them fall.

"Even if I love you too much," he said, "please don't kill me."

I was probably awake by the time I tried to answer. He and I began to disappear, leaving last the faint sound of the song.

I sat up and looked inside the empty hand where my son receded, even from the memory of touch. When there was nothing left at all I began to cry, as he had not.

CHAPTER ONE

HELLO, DARKNESS

I spent my day off in my room. I didn't have any obligations. I didn't have to be anywhere. Besides, the cold morning rain just kept on coming. I had no reason to go out at all.

I had a reason, though, in the evening. I ran out of Gabu's dog food. Gabu is a good-natured basset. She's not generally fussy, but if there's one thing she is picky about, it's her food.

She'll only eat the mega-strength-enhancing, immuno-enhanced, super-enriched, worldwide dog breeders' choice, organically preserved *Bajidu*—from *bajídùlièquán*, Mandarin for basset hound. Gabu likes no other. She might try giving lesser brands a sniff, perhaps a few polite bites, but the rest will dry up and harden in her bowl, like it always does.

Sure, I'm indulging my dog in this matter, but I really think Gabu deserves it. So I told her, "You wait here. I'll go pick up some Bajidu for you."

Gabu answered with a few understanding taps of the tail. I left my apartment and went down to the Volvo, turning the key to let myself be carried into the downtown district on auto-drive.

It was drizzling all over the city. The pedestrians passed before me as flat as three dimensions can be, and the car's radar sidestepped every one in nimble high pitch as the visible light of the headlamps blurred to impotence in airy water. Red plasma writhed against white fluorescent ache, as rows of Chinese *hanzi* marched straight on the windshield, leapt, and then were gone in the rearview, having spoken for their CHONG SAN SUN STORE, represented their BIG

RED PUSSY CO., promised their MONEY FRIENDSHIP LOVE, and even alluded to their FRAGRANT MERCY. It was like a dream—if such a dream wasn't another cliché.

I was approaching a landmark—the ruins of the steeple, known as the battle building. It was a standing wreck, its largely intact exterior concealing the damage from the bomb within. Where its ruin blocked the light a huge arc lamp buzzed like a single great fly, rubbing pale blue sparks off its legs into the shadows.

As I turned the corner of the steeple, I suddenly heard the siren of a patrol car. Should I link my e-brain to the police dispatch system? I hesitated a moment—but then the siren sound grew distant and vanished.

Now I was finding the noise of the windshield wiper irritating and switched on the muse—my radio. Lee Morgan's trumpet, pouring the moan of "I'm a Fool to Want You" into the car. It was reminding me of something…

Before I managed to recall what it was, I reached my destination and the music stopped.

I had on a leather jacket, but it wasn't the kind you'd regret wearing in the rain. I took my time walking from the parking lot to the convenience store.

It was deserted this late at night. They had poor inventory. The drifting hologram ads in the aisles had no viewers, and just as often, there were no products on the empty shelves to pass. The sight was oddly desolate, reminding me of the homeless wandering through the alleys of the city. The impression wasn't merely maudlin. Real stores were on the wane as cybermarkets flourished.

I looked for Bajidu in the pet food section, where there wasn't much to scan. There was none to be found. It wasn't necessarily a popular brand, but that inventory system, again…

Then I looked for a human clerk. I couldn't find one of those either. So I called upon the hologram projector, which perked up with a little song that went, *"If you want a drink, la la la, drink Pepsi."*

"No," I said. "I'm looking for *Bajidu*. The dog food. You had it in last month, but I can't find it now."

The projector was a new model; it had the capacity to sound disappointed. "Oh. Is that all?" There was a brief pause, searching perhaps. "We no longer stock Bajidu. There isn't much demand for fresh foods like that. They spoil too fast. Maybe you should try some *dry* dog food, sir? They last and they provide your pet with the nutrition it requires."

"My basset hound doesn't eat dry food. She'll only eat fresh food. In fact, the only food she'll eat is Bajidu. It's your responsibility to meet the customer's demands."

"Dogs aren't our customers. It's their humans who have the money. And as such, we urge humans to provide their pets with dry food. As I've already mentioned to you, sir, dry food is more cost effective, it lasts longer, and it meets all nutritional needs. We're your neighborhood retailer. And it's *our* responsibility to advocate products we value."

I wouldn't say it had been wrong so far. But the idea of a convenience store robot having its way with a human— a cyborg of one, to be strictly technical about it—was too humiliating. I decided to stand up for myself.

"Bassets have their own preferences. As an owner I'd like to satisfy my dog. Providing satisfaction for my dog gratifies *me*. You'd understand if you had a dog of your own."

"A dog of my own? I'm only a *hologram projector*, sir. But even were I human, would I share my life with a dog? I doubt it. I'd want to share it with a woman. I'd be so busy with her I'd have no time for a pet—that much I can assure you, sir.

Why don't you spend *your* time with a woman, instead of with a dog?"

"What difference would that make? She'd still want the fresh food."

The projector's LCDs began to flash rapidly. I didn't presume to understand its body language, but I suspect it found that pretty funny.

"So you'd still end up down here at the store, with me trying to talk you into kibble," it said, still flashing.

"Probably."

"You can't always get what you want."

"That's right." I nodded. "You can't."

"If you want a drink," it sang, "drink Pepsi."

I ended up following the projector's recommendations in detail and bought five different brands of dry food. I knew it was a pointless effort on the Gabu front. She wouldn't go near that stuff. I just wanted to show some respect for that remarkable projector.

Out the door it was still raining. I got wet walking towards the parking lot. Water doesn't bother me, and the groceries would be dry under the leather coat.

I stopped before I reached the car. I focused my eyes and stared ahead.

There were two figures hunched over the windshield. One gave a big impression, and I am 190 centimeters tall.

The other man was small, a little over 160 cm, it seemed. There was nothing distinct about the small man at all, lurking in the bigger man's shadow. It was odd how I looked at him, and yet he hardly made an impression.

I picked up what he was whispering to the big man. "Not yet. Don't access it yet."

Yet? What were they waiting for? What were they

accessing? I had no idea. I didn't even want to know. The only thing I was interested in was whether they were tampering with my car. That was all. I didn't care about anything else.

The security sensor didn't go off. Which meant they weren't. Now they were wiping the windshield with a rag meticulously. I could tell their state from their shabby looks. A shopping cart stood beside them.

The tall man looked up at me and gave me a generous smile. "Hey, you're late. I thought you might not come back at all."

I could never forget this encounter. The first time I met him. Which meant...

This was only a mistaken memory. That couldn't be. A hallucination again. But again, that certainty of detail. "The Sound of Silence" playing in the background when I first met Ando. Whether it was "The Sound of Silence" or "I'm a Fool to Want You," whether it was true or false, the memory was built to stay somewhere in my head—

The night, the rain, Ando, and Simon and Garfunkel's voices sadly drifting through the abyss of the night, and the sound of Lee Morgan's trumpet...

— 2 —

At first I thought it was a trivial encounter. We met, spoke, and then parted ways. I figured it wouldn't take me more than three minutes to forget it all. That's how it usually goes. But this turned out differently. Ando became unforgettable.

I don't mean to say he was unforgettable in a sentimental way. That wasn't the case. My e-brain has been reinitialized several times. But my memory of Ando has always been saved in the buffer zone. You might say that Ando has become *physically* unforgettable.

And yet my encounter with him was very ordinary. His voice when he spoke hardly struck me as remarkable. To be honest, I couldn't understand why I'd remember this...

"It's a nice evening." That's what Ando said. "Don't you think?"

It was ludicrous. I looked at Ando's face, sighed, and shook my head. "It's raining, man."

"That's true, it is raining." Ando chuckled. "So?"

"You're saying, so what?"

"Yeah."

"You don't usually say it's nice out when it's raining."

"You don't?"

"You don't." I nodded. "When it's raining, it's not nice out."

"Under normal circumstances."

"Yeah, usually."

"Is that so?"

"Yeah. Besides..."

"Besides?"

"There isn't much point in cleaning a window in the middle of a rainy night."

"You mean, 'under normal circumstances'?"

"That's right." Now the chuckle was mine. "Under normal circumstances."

I took the keys out of my pocket and released the car lock. With a swift nod, I signaled him to get out of my away.

Of course, I wasn't being hostile. In fact, I felt somewhat friendly towards him. But whether I felt friendly or not, this was just a passing encounter. He had nothing to do with me. That's how things were supposed to be, but...

The man complied. He grasped his shopping cart and

took several steps back. The cart's wheels were gleaming from the rain. The flash off them felt like a pang in the heart. A *pang*, a momentary guilt...

I nodded to make him go away as if I couldn't be bothered wasting words on him. I'd give him some change once I put the bag of dog food on the seat. Enough change to buy a meal at the convenience store. I would get in the car, drive off, and forget about him. Then this man would vanish from my life for good—like a useless program deleted from a PC.

Was that right? Whether it was or not, that's how people lead their lives. Besides, ever since I lost Motoko I've been a recluse, not getting involved with others. I don't love anyone now. I can't. I don't intend to. The only exception is Gabu.

I hesitated for a moment. But then, my body proceeded naturally without interruption. I opened the car door and put the bag on the seat. I turned to the man, took some change from my pocket, and offered it to him. I examined his face.

The man stared at the coins in my hand, then looked up at me. He concentrated on the coins again. Maybe it was from living on the streets—his face was tanned and rugged. But his cheeks were surprisingly well defined. They almost looked young—they were young. That was when I realized how young he really was. He must have been in his early twenties, no more. A troubled look flashed across his face.

He looked up at me again. Then he quietly said, "I am Ando."

There was a pause.

"I can't take alms from an anonymous person. Don't you agree? So. I am Ando."

"I'm Batou." I said quickly. "I'm called Batou."

"Pleased to meet you, Batou."

"Likewise, Ando."

Ando laughed. It was such a vulnerable, open laugh. He took the coins from my hand, so guilelessly. He looked me straight in the eye.

"Right now, I'm down on my luck, but someday I'll be back on my feet again. Then I'm going to return your favor. I hope you can count on me for that."

"Of course, I will." I smiled. "I mean it. I'm counting on you."

And that ended the accidental encounter I had with this stranger at night. Wouldn't want to give him the impression I was a good man. I'd end up disappointing him on that score. My practical supply of goodwill is very limited. It bottoms out quick.

I slid onto my seat. The car door closed automatically... and I left Ando behind. His existence was automatically deleted from my mind. I wasn't supposed to recall him.

$$- 3 -$$

I gripped the steering wheel, which activates the auto-drive mode. My e-brain was now linked to its program. I could see the GPS map inside my head. Its indicator began to flash. With a blink I moved the map to the precise location.

These things all occurred automatically. You're not even aware it's taking place. It's almost like breathing. Something a human rarely checks—except when all of a sudden, they aren't breathing right.

And that's how I suddenly felt, right now. On the rare occasion that I start up a PC, I've been able to *sense* if it's been hacked. That's what this also felt like.

Someone had entered through the car's navigation system.

My e-brain's being hacked. Someone's looking inside me ... That's how my thoughts went. A virus ... I called up a neural chart with another blink, trying to find it, apply an automatic vaccine. The scan was 60 percent complete within several fractions of a second, which is how long it took me to run out of time. I froze up.

Then the car burst forward with a roar, tires screeching against the pavement. It was too late to try and lock the brakes. Sparks shot up from the tires and lanced down like the Niagara. I was racing through a waterfall of fire.

I tried shifting my e-brain to multi-processing and manual power mode. Even cyborgs are prone to making this type of mistake. When the e-brain is linked to a machine that runs out of control, a cyborg can panic and force its own e-brain to shut down.

It was just an error in judgment on my part.

A flesh human is hardly ever aware of his or her temporal region—their working memory—or prefrontal region—the operating system. That's why they end up consolidating all their brain functions into an abstraction like the soul. Conversely, a cyborg is prone to making errors of an entirely different type. Unaware that the brain is a part of himself, the cyborg ends up *handling* his e-brain like a notepad.

That's how I made the critical mistake of shutting down my brain in order to switch to manual mode. A human needs his brain even when he's only swinging a hammer. A cyborg shutting down his is no different from a human losing consciousness.

I would never deliberately do something so stupid, but the results were the same. The multi-processing came in too late. I was severed from my brain.

Now my backup system activated.

There's another crucial difference between a cyborg's brain and a human's. An e-brain doesn't secrete neurotransmitters. Functional reactions such as "excitement" and "fear" caused by chemical substances in the organic mind are controlled calculations in the e-brain. Unlike the human version, there's no "play" in an e-brain. That probably explains why we have no subconscious—and therefore no "surface" consciousness. There are virtual forms you can install, but...

Androids don't dream of electric sheep. You see, they don't dream at all.

The neural patterns formed every moment on the e-brain's crystal structure are reducible to a simple program. Its correlation equations are entered into a flat matrix. Both literally and metaphorically, a cyborg has no highs and lows. Its consciousness has no depth.

Therefore, a cyborg cannot normally be in a dazed state, like the kind you have upon awakening. The consciousness is either on or off. There is no gray zone. It has its advantages.

And its greatest drawback is that the moment consciousness is off, the body ceases to exist. Humans have reflexes hardwired into their spine and brainstem and endocrine system that will act without conscious thought. But a cyborg can't do anything with his body without being conscious of it. Something that doesn't exist can't act.

No "fight or flight" response, no jerking a hand away from heat. A cyborg has no choice but to keep his head in an emergency. He has none of the simple instincts evolved over billennia by organic life.

When consciousness fails, he has a simulation. The backup, to be technical as can be: a correlation equation matrix to produce excitation patterns, rewritten as a virtual Gestalt structure.

The effect: oddly, simply to impose a virtual form of the three-dimensional awareness humans normally possess, *trompe-l'œil* for the mind's eye. This provides a temporary subconscious. The designers call it meta-awareness.

In it I could act.

What a state to be in.

$$- 4 -$$

My runaway car—a special model, customized by my unit, Domestic Security Section 9. Armored glass, EMP shielded, anti-CBW.

I don't know about electromagnetic pulse and biochemical warfare. Frankly, those issues have never come up on the commute. But the glass is no boast. It's stopped anti-tank weapons. This heap's only real forte is its brute strength.

It's heavy, heavier than it looks. The brakes and power train are enhanced, too, so the fact rarely matters. It mattered now, as the hardened front ripped across a line of cars as I hurtled down the parking lot.

A chain reaction: sedans crashing into each other, economy models flipping up into the air like baby carts. The din from five flavors of car alarm was deafening, until the spark shower hit the sprays of gasoline and explosions buried the treble under bass.

Somewhere in the back of a frozen mind was the datum that 58 percent of cars still use gasoline. It was one of those ask-the-public surveys you take with a grain of salt, but odd how the last few seconds of fire had made a believer out of me. How sad indeed that environmental preservation keeps taking a backseat to profits.

More sad at the moment was the fact Section 9 set no good example—for this car I was stuck in also burns gas. In fact, it would be happy to burn it fast and hot and explode just like my fellow citizens' rides. I had to do something immediately. But...

What *could* I do? How could I get out of this bind?

Between the second ticks of my fear lay this: without my e-brain, I had no option but to think this through in my meta-aware mode. It couldn't even be *called* thinking, or even reflexes. These were simulated reflexes.

A cyborg lacks dedicated involuntary muscles. The concept is irrelevant to their architecture. All a cyborg's muscles are voluntary.

But it would be impossible (yes, even for a cyborg) to lead a normal life if you were constantly aware of all your muscle functions, artificial even as they are. Having to keep track of your heartbeat? How about your bowel movements? Annoying at minimum, more like ridiculous. A subprogram for involuntary action is written into a cyborg instead, switch-relayed within the main programming. Voluntary muscles in the guise of involuntary muscles. It's basically a Trojan horse. It's merely designed to supercede my cognition. However...

With the loss of my e-brain and activation of my virtual unconscious, the involuntary nerve sub-program took over the main program, canceling out any voluntary action.

I didn't have control over my body. My consciousness was isolated.

I couldn't be certain, but someone was very likely hacking into my skull.

Therefore, even if I were who I was, I was no longer me.

And yet I haven't even mentioned the real trouble.

The hacker could turn off my power supply whenever he wanted. My life was literally in his hands. I had to find a way to escape or I'd be dead from either fire or a mere flick of the switch.

The owner pulls the plug on his refrigerator and shoves it outside on collection day. He's thinking about the next model, the one with the improved ice cubes, and never stops to think on his old fridge's feelings.

Of course, I can tell you. The refrigerator is very upset.

I don't want to be scrapped. Unlike the fridge, a cyborg has his resources.

— 5 —

The backup system initialized an involuntary muscle contraction in cycles. It's an emergency device to generate startup power in my body, in turn recharging my internal battery.

Your spinal cord controls many of your reflexes. Mine serves another function. It is used for auxiliary power storage. If a cyborg loses both its e-brain and all power, it can't be rebooted. It will have to be reinitialized.

The manual says the auxiliary lasts eight minutes, so better to assume it's really four. An especially pessimistic fellow might cut that to three.

I only had three minutes, then, to retrieve my runaway brain from the hacker, or I might as well be thrown away.

If this were a hard-boiled movie, the car seat would be the electric chair, the seatbelt strapping me in. But I'm not the kind the governor would pardon. Worst of all, I didn't know for sure if I was guilty or innocent.

All I saw was the executioner's hand, waiting to throw the switch.

The battery indicator blinked into vision, counting down in hundredths of seconds—false generosity, like handing someone a pile of slivers.

Good old meta-awareness now spent one shaving of it upon an old saying, one they have in the English language—*how time flies*.

Power. I could move.

I began moving. On battery, in unconscious mode, I linked to the navigation system, making an internal backup of the control. I could only hope the process wouldn't take more than, say, thirty of the seconds I had left to live.

By now my car had bashed every vehicle in range, like a pub brawler—smashed, burned, and toppled them over. My section director, Aramaki, might not get out of this mess alive either. There was that heart attack he'd likely have when the bill for the civil suits came up...

...which I could worry about some time when my own car wasn't a hurtling spear of fire that vector brakes and a steering wheel could not easily stop.

I knew something that could, though. The steel fence at the end of this long, long street—nice and solid, with its ten-centimeter steel posts and high-tension current.

There was a certain irony, I admit, in trying to use my battery power to avoid merging with more electricity than I could ever need. And it was just some urban dweller's anti-theft measure, after all. Even that dingy convenience store was wired like Fort Knox with nasty things to go off, had I decided to take the hologram's advice without paying. It's either that or be a pushover for robbery.

It's just the city.

The fence threw out its sparks from far down the avenue, greeting those from my own Volvo like a mating of fireflies. It was a pretty sight to no one concerned.

The Volvo was tough. And I'm pretty tough myself. But I would hit that juiced-up steel at 200 kilometers per hour and that would just about do it for both of us. Smashed and roasted would be the terms, like the things in your holiday dinner.

Installation complete. It hadn't taken thirty seconds. It had taken one minute, thirteen.

I really wanted someone to pray for me, for I had to complete everything within a couple minutes. My mind leapt to heaven now, to grasp the angel of a GPS satellite. Forty seconds more to wait, and two klicks closer to the end.

– 6 –

With less than a minute left of power, I was connected and counting on confusion from above.

GPS, like the Internet and other things we can't live without, comes to you courtesy of the U.S. Department of Defense. It was originally a military-only system. In fact, it's controlled by their Air Force Space Command. They like to do a little thing on occasion called SA—Selective Availability, where they deliberately scramble the GPS broadcast, throwing off the accuracy of the navigation signal for civilian users. Don't ask me why. It's supposed to be a security measure.

Not by much in the global scheme of things—a block or two off at the most. But even a few meters' worth of wiggle in my auto-drive would go a long way towards my car smacking into something less lethal, like the nice brick walls that lined the avenue.

It would just take another forty seconds for the SA to kick in.

The red light was blinking on my battery as the auto-drive tried to adjust, fed the new, uncertain signal.

And nothing happened. Straight on for the fence, now a few hundred meters away.

IN THESE MINUTES, many small different hopes had burst with cheap drama, like firecrackers. That's a life. But since Motoko has been gone, I've known that there is only one big despair, and whether in the real or made mind, it always teaches the same thing.

In a few more moments a loud or quiet ending would come. Once my battery was depleted, my fast body and my awareness of it would disappear. This subconscious, already virtual, would become indistinguishable in the void, infinite and empty. An oblivion heaven, ruled by a deus ex machina.

I expected to meet her there again.

—*Major, I . . .*

I WHAT? WHAT was *I* trying to say? I don't know. Without knowing I would . . .

At three minutes and twenty seconds, my battery failed and my subconscious blinked out—

—and my e-brain returned to me and my power supply was back up to 100 percent.

The SA operation had disabled the auto-drive entirely. It could no longer maintain the connection with the e-brain, and hence it could no longer cut me off from it.

I howled with glee and gripped the wheel with my superhuman hands. You know, I always liked to believe I could do anything with them.

Of course, I couldn't, because the wide fence filled the windshield now.

I clenched my teeth so my jaw wouldn't crack, and slid down so the steering wheel wouldn't slam into my chest, and locked my legs so something else completely useless they told me in training wouldn't stop this from happening when I—

Ando leaped out of nowhere and jumped between the car and the fence.

I had hundredths of a second left sufficient to be dumbfounded. He should have been crushed between the car and the fence, deader even than me.

He should have been, but, you see, safety regulations forbade it. The one built into every car along with its seatbelts, the one which says if those nimble front sensors detect a pedestrian, the car *must move to avoid the pedestrian.*

The Volvo skidded to the left. The tires spun, whirring so loud it grated against my ears. A very laudable obeisance to the law my car made—until the higher law of physics claimed jurisdiction. One side tipped up and the car flipped over. And over.

My VISUAL SCREEN spun round like a gyro until the field locked on again and I managed to see straight. But the last thing I heard in one ear was a light pop, and with depressing cyborg certainty determined it was the snap of one of my semicircular canals.

Dual mode front airbag, side airbag, inflatable windshield curtain—the whole nine, and still I thudded and whudded in the fierceness of the roll. I vaguely registered that if I had been human, the bags would just by now be playing a merry game of toss the corpse.

Now the car had stopped spinning and started skating—sideward down the pavement. A fresh crop of sparks mixed with the blooming flame and I was back in the good old days of mere mortal danger, instead of certain death. *Get out of the car.* But I was stuck in this unnatural position, plus sealed in by the pretensioner which had locked the seatbelt. Another safety measure, in an evening full of them. I had a knife in one of my pants pockets. And I couldn't reach it in that position just noted.

The vehicle wiring went. The dashboard caught fire with ropy black smoke. It would only be a matter of moments before the gasoline tank itself ignited. The car would turn into a ball of flames.

I was in a refreshing new form of trouble.

— 7 —

There was no sign of things looking up. In fact, the forecast was for bad, followed by worse.

My body reacted reflexive*ly*—that adverb form, again. My upper body bound into the overturned car, I lifted up my legs. And then I kicked in the head deck like a bull.

The head deck cover cracked off into the scattering sparks.

My sawed-off shotgun was hidden there. Five shells inside, each packed with nine double-ought slugs. My arms went for it in a monkey grab and I flipped the safety and cocked with a ratchet. There's something about a gun to use that also puts me on automatic. It's not a cyborg thing.

I already had damage to one ear, and this was going to be loud inside the closed vehicle. I dropped my hearing sensitivity to ten percent normal and put my finger on the trigger.

The world, even with all its trouble, was nearly silent. Now the sparks scattered without hiss or fizz, like luminous snow. An error in my e-brain made me hear Lee Morgan, however faint. The trumpet was no more than a dog whimper.

I thrust the barrel at the door still skating on the ground.

I fired. Again. Again. And again.

The strobe of the gun flash, and the recoil! Secured to the seat, I couldn't compensate, so each shot did a steel-toed boot into my shoulder. I couldn't dodge the shell casings either, and they singed my brows. On the fourth shot a strange thing happened.

The flipped-over armored car began to magically float into the air.

It had been a good trick. The car door is specially designed to provide an escape for passengers in a crisis. True, the door was resting on the road. But when it does open in emergency mode, it's with the power of an ejector seat. The action lifted the car body off the asphalt like a jack.

I felt the thud against the ground. For a split second my body was weightless. If I hadn't been strapped in by the seatbelt, I'd have smacked against the ceiling. Then the car landed. Upright again.

The tires had grip. Now was my chance. I slammed on the brakes—and they locked.

The car spun halfway. The centrifugal force spun the world around me. My visual stabilizer couldn't adjust.

As I spun around I thought I caught again in the whirl-round a glimpse of oblivion or death. Must it be defined by numbers, for a cyborg? It would shatter like a broken mirror then...

The vision settled itself into a line of shopping carts flying apart. Several of them traced a snake in the pouring rain, splashing against the pavement.

My car had crashed into the carts arranged in the back of a parking lot, pushing down a dozen meters' worth as it scattered and knocked them aside.

Then the car stopped and it was finally over.

THE SEATBELT SNAPPED OFF. My visual regained its horizontal alignment. I brought my hearing back up to normal. But there was nothing to see through the kaleidoscope of the cracked windshield, nor was there anything to hear. The parking lot was deserted.

I could only hear the quiet rain. It sounded very distant, even though it was all around.

Now that I could move, I couldn't bring myself to. I didn't even want to move my fingers.

This was another sound of silence.

I think that I probably wanted to believe I really had died just now, dead tired, exhausted from existing in this state. I was tired of *being*—a cyborg, controlled by "my" e-brain. I'd grown weary of that: myself.

I feel this sometimes. No, all the time, though I'm often not the guy to notice it.

It doesn't seem strange to find solace in my own death. Once I die, after all, I'll be liberated from both electronic brain and mechanical body, and then, I might even meet Motoko. That's right, somewhere beyond this world...

Of course, this thought was fully tangible, as much they say as any sweet dream.

– 8 –

Back here. Whether you're flesh human or cyborg, you can't rest easy as long as you're alive. There's no place to go beyond your world. And my grip on reality was gradually returning. It was the reality I had to accept, even if it was pleasant as eating sand.

The rain tapped persistently, straight from the roof of the world down to my head. You're linked to all this, it said, to something so desolate it made me want to cry.

And in my little corner of it, someone had hacked into my car's computer. Who had done it? And why?

My e-brain had been severed from me because it was connected to the car. That was what made the car lose control. But that was only a result, and an unforeseen result, perhaps. I actually doubted that crashing the car had been the purpose.

Did the hacker do it because he knew I was part of Domestic Security Unit Section 9? Or was he just the kind who, bored, chooses his targets randomly?

And if not to cause a crash, then why hack into a car's navigation system?

I pondered this in such a daze that I didn't notice motion before me.

Through the smashed windshield, its thousand cracks filled with rain, a figure was visible. It took me a couple minutes before I realized it was Ando. No, my brain still wasn't functioning properly.

What is Ando doing?

The answer was obvious. Ando was rearranging the shopping carts. That was all. Nothing more than that. Except he was engrossed in the strange task, working as if possessed.

Now I was truly surrounded by mystery. Why was it important for him to do this? Did he even have a reason? How could he?

And yet there he was with diligence, drenched in the rain. His movements had an automatic nature of their own. In light of everything, it was perverse. Something was wrong with him.

That didn't matter. I had to thank Ando. In fact, I couldn't thank him enough. He had saved my life, or whatever it is that I have.

A ghost inside a cyborg.

And my e-brain echoed Ando's words.

Right now, I'm down on my luck, but someday I'll be back on my feet again. Then I'm going to return your favor. I hope you can count on me for that...Right now, I'm down on my luck, but someday I'll be back on my feet again. Then I'm going to return your favor. I hope you can count on me for that...Right now, I'm down on my luck...

THIS YOUNG MAN ANDO was loyal. He had returned my favor almost instantaneously, and with interest. Now I was the one who owed him.

I got out of the car. I walked up to him.

I realized then that Ando surely was in no normal state.

He was dividing the pile of shopping cars into rows on both sides. He did it with such determination. What could this be?

He might be acting according to a scheme that made good sense to him. In fact the pattern looked strangely familiar, but I wasn't able to recall what it was...

"Thanks for saving me. I owe you one," I said to Ando.

Ando turned around. He looked at me. His face was another desolation.

Even after he looked, he still didn't say a word. I wasn't sure he was actually seeing me. I think he saw the rain. And himself drenched in the rain. He saw his solitude.

— 9 —

"Are you all right?" I asked. "What are you doing?"

Ando gave a gaze. Then he asked me to find it. He sounded tense.

"Find?" I knit my brows. "Find what?"

"A memory." Ando said. "My own memory."

"A memory? You're searching for a memory. Did you lose your memory?"

"That's what a memory is, right? Something you lose. But…"

"But what?"

"There are memories you mustn't lose. Don't you have ones like that?"

I didn't say anything, because of course I did.

But I couldn't share them, even with Ando. I couldn't share them with anyone.

"So it was a memory I wasn't supposed to lose. But I ended up losing it…him…"

His eyes wandered uneasily. As if searching…but there was only the rain. Only the rain coming down, pouring and pouring. Nothing besides that.

"'Him'? What did you do to *him?* What is this memory you should have kept?"

I was trying to get his attention, really, rather than

expecting an actual answer. Given my personal aversion to "reality," I had no right to say this, but I wanted to bring Ando back here.

Ando was in another place.

Did Ando hit his head when he dove for my car? I don't want to make any simple excuses, but I knew it wasn't like that…Even when I first met Ando there was something ethereal about him. He seemed too pure, too innocent to be flesh of this world.

"I killed him. I killed the memory…"

"'Him,' who? Who are you talking about? What happened to your memory?"

"I killed it."

I asked, "Was it a memory you weren't supposed to kill?"

"I wasn't supposed to kill that memory. I wasn't supposed to kill him. And yet…" Ando's face contorted slightly.

"And yet…?"

"I ended up killing him," said Ando. "I ended up forgetting."

His was the face of the son in my dream. *Even if I love you too much, please don't kill me.* I felt a slight oscillation, something akin to guilt.

Ando took a step towards me and then his chin drooped. He fell forward to the wet ground. If I hadn't held out my arms to him, he would have split his head against the pavement.

I stood there and held Ando in the rain forever. No, that's wrong. It was for only ten minutes. Why would I recall it later as having lasted so long? It was because I only knew that young man briefly, but the *memory* of him was unforgettable. Probably I knew that would be true.

Ando gave me a blank look. His eyes were filled with nothing aside from darkness.

Or was it not dark but empty…the unreal sense, the void, the e-brain spinning off, outside…I had been close myself, not long ago.

I could tell Ando did not have an e-brain like me, but the one he was born with. It had a prosthetic, however—a crystal device which linked partial e-brain lobes with his neuronal tissue.

I couldn't say at a glance just how much inside his head had been replaced, but one thing was sure—at some point in the past, Ando must have suffered a serious brain injury. Because unless the damage was severe, a doctor wouldn't even consider trying to fix it with this kind of implant. Original function might be restored in such a case, but not original personality.

That may be why Ando became a homeless man.

The thought occurred to me. But it was none of my business. I had no desire to get involved with anyone, no matter who it was. Ando was meant to be a passing stranger. He was not supposed to matter.

I had already called the paramedic service. An EMT team would be here for Ando within five minutes. But I knew he would be dead by then.

Tilt your head back, and your eyes will appear to look down. Tilt your head down and they appear to look up. Appear to, because of course they look neither up nor down, but instead maintain your vision on the same spot to keep you oriented. It happens without you having to think about it. Otherwise you couldn't do so much as walk straight. I have a visual stabilizer that corrects my eyes with my motions—but humans have this thing called the vestibulo-ocular reflex.

Except Ando didn't have it, not anymore. When I moved his head back his eyes moved with his head—not like a human, but like a doll. The reflex is in your brain stem, where the most basic functions of life reside. Its absence meant very soon he could not be saved. There was an unknown point of no return, and I knew it would be within those next five minutes. I had to stop him from vanishing away.

This would be a peaceful death for him, I thought, and it was meaningless and consoling. But I had the option to revive him, which may or may not be meaningless. It was definitely not consoling.

It would put me in deadly danger once again, I thought, as I began the process.

We think of consciousness as something of the higher brain, but it doesn't happen there alone—only as part of a constant connectivity between the brainstem and the cortical, higher brain. People in a persistent vegetative state have an impaired connection. Awareness is an interactive process between the most primitive and advanced places within you. A cyborg that knows it exists as a ghost in a shell is *conscious* of consciousness in a way few in flesh ever are or can be.

Whatever might be wrong with Ando's stem—well, I'm no brain surgeon.

But when it comes to consciousness, I am the man. I am the specialist.

THE RETINA IS A cyborg's interface. The same holds true for a human whose brain is partially electronic. Manual operation of the e-brain can be conducted through an infrared light link. If the victim is unconscious, then you can remote control their e-brain by looking into their eyes.

That's exactly what I did. I looked into Ando's eyes. I switched my visual sensor to infrared light mode. I linked

Ando's e-brain section with my own e-brain and initialized it. The danger...

All the data is backed up, and the discrete functions of the mind are re-installed automatically. But the big picture you try to make here is no less than the reconstruction of a wound and folded bud, the gestalt from which a personality emerges—an individual...

And you lose your own consciousness while the process runs. The e-brain goes into a state of innocence.

It goes somewhere, but where is that?

ANDO'S FACE IN my visual field began to fade. Then a gray field tinged with blue appeared as the initialization began. A blinking dot stands for me. Otherwise I don't exist.

The minimal memory needed to maintain *Batou* remains in the buffer zone so it won't be erased during the initialization of *Ando*.

The buffer memory load is very small. So only the minimum needed to secure an identity is allowed. The os will decide your essentials in this process. The cyborg has no conscious say in what to take and what to leave.

You're never allowed to determine what defines you.

The gray zone for initialization changed to white. White noise. Whiteout, the rain. Now I saw the rain, tapping against the car windshield.

I felt a strange sense of loss, an interrupt. I felt strange. What was I doing? I asked myself.

I WAS SITTING in the rear seat of a taxi, staring at the windshield. Raindrops streaked across the glass.

The taxi was driving through the city. A branch of rain-drops shook, flowing down ahead of me at a slight angle. I found I could measure the speed of the car by their descent. Some curved and then dropped straight, making question marks. The lights of the city were no help. They were blurred in cobalt blue.

There was no point in vision. The taxi was being navigated. Some cabs still have a driver for show, but not this one.

The muse was playing "I'm a Fool to Want You." The trumpet melody now fairly rang.

The music in these cabs was customer's choice. Did I select it, though? I really couldn't remember.

An ambulance blared against the brass, somewhere in the city. Were the color gangs rioting again? Or maybe it was the Asian mafia, stirring up trouble...

I wonder if Section 9 has been...

I take a look out the window.

But I can't see anything. I don't understand it at all. There's only the rain. And the sharp silhouette of the needle, the spire of the battle building, trying to knit the heavens to the earth.

And I remembered now. I went out to buy dog food for Gabu. Gabu will only eat Bajidu...

Hadn't I done this before? Of course I had—my dog likes to eat, after all. I put my unease at this repetition aside. I ignored it.

I told the taxi's auto-drive, "My convenience store—on the corner. I need to stop there."

The console lamps blinked in response. It was the computer equivalent of a grunt. Rainy nights like this were a drag for everybody.

What do you know, they had it in stock. I bought several

boxes and returned to my cab. The hologram projector flashed its lights for my attention, but I passed it by.

It was best to avoid projectors trying to make a sales pitch. They were nothing but trouble. Nowadays, there were even false ones in the stores, like crooked carny games, trying to scam you into buying charms to conjure spirits.

$$- \text{IO} -$$

I returned to my apartment, opened my door, and called for my dog.

Gabu is loyal and lazy. Of course, calling her loyal is a compliment. And when I say she's lazy, it's only a fact, not an insult. I would never put that dog down.

I love Gabu, and it comes from all the things just to like. Gabu's round pupils. Gabu's wet nose. Most of all, Gabu's zesty appetite. No matter what, Gabu never loses her lust for grub.

She always wags her tail and welcomes me whenever I come home. And we both know what's coming next: a steady series of barks as she waits for me to fill up her bowl with Bajidu. Then she'll plow her muzzle into it and shove furrows of food onto the kitchen floor. It's a daily ritual.

But for some reason, Gabu didn't greet me when I entered the apartment that night. In fact, instead of entering the kitchen, she backed away. It was very odd. She was whimpering sadly. What had happened to my poor dog?

"What's wrong?" I tilted my head to inquire. "It's your dinner. Don't you want your dinner?"

The doorbell rang. I was worried about Gabu, but then I couldn't ignore a visitor. I hardly ever had any. In fact I never had any, except for the postman, a dedicated android.

I turned towards the door. I didn't forget to reassure Gabu, though.

"This is your favorite. Bajidu. Why won't you eat it? You shouldn't be so fussy—"

I opened the door.

Of course, it was a delivery—something I had ordered over the Internet.

An instant message window opened in my e-brain. It was Togusa, a fellow Unit 9 officer. I signaled the postman to wait while I took care of the message.

We don't exchange greetings. That's not a sign of intimacy. It's just with all we've been through, they seem so futile.

So Togusa cut to the chase.

"We have another case of a gynoid attacking its owners. The husband's dead. The wife's in serious condition."

It doesn't take much to guess a *gynoid* is a girl android. The Locus Solus corporation plans a fall launch for their mass-produced gynoid model, dubbed "Hadaly." In preparation, Hadaly prototypes were provided free of charge to contractors for testing.

But there'd been a bloody flurry of accidents where Hadalys attacked their new owners. Six cases so far—pretty serious. Still and all…

"So what," I said. "These gynoid incidents have nothing to do with Section 9. We're counterterrorism."

"For now they don't." Togusa grimaced at what he said next. "But the director doesn't want to rule out some kind of political angle. It's only being considered, but eventually he might just put us on the case. I'm giving you fair warning."

"Understood." I ended the communication. Back to the android.

"Don't you care?" he asked.

"About what?

"Your dog just went out. Is that okay?"

"What…"

For a moment, I didn't understand what he meant. I only gazed at him.

I believe that was when my e-brain was fully restored, and I could see clearly. Too late, though, for me.

A new window opened. This one kept replaying a video of Gabu slipping past me, going into the hall. Her tail swept the floor sadly behind her. Her head drooped as she slowly pattered away.

I never, ever saw Gabu like that.

I ran into the hall and called her name.

I called, and called, and kept on calling.

From that day on, I called for her.

CHAPTER TWO

SPLIT THE NIGHT

A week went by since Gabu disappeared.

It was a very, very long week. It felt like a month to me. Or a year, a decade. Or longer.

In fact, the passage of time is absolutely meaningless for someone like me who's lost their dog. It doesn't matter how many more zeroes you add to the first. They will not distance you from it.

What is solitude? You don't have to pour through the classics. No need to check out Tennessee Williams's plays.

Just ask me, and this is what I'd tell you: solitude is nothing more than an unfilled bowl left on a kitchen floor. That's the concrete form it takes.

I couldn't bring myself to put her bowl away. I was scared that to do so would make her absence permanent. I couldn't even bear it. So on the floor it stayed, and I filled it with solitude.

Leftover dog food stales and hardens. It's funny how solitude stays fresh, as if it refills itself. Loneliness lasts in a way that love can't seem to.

I lost Motoko, and now I lost Gabriel. And now I can't forget that I lost them. Those who've never caught the scent are fortunate. And of course, they don't exist. They are, who are lonely.

IT'S NOT LIKE I spent the week moping. How could I sit still, with Gabu gone?

I combed her usual routes. I contacted the local SPCA. I posted Gabu's photo on the city's "Missing Dog" site. Six-year-old female basset hound. Chubby. Friendly. Voracious appetite. Lazy...

And strictly speaking, it was against regulations, but I took one of the police dogs to track her.

The dog was an extremely dependable and faithful shepherd called John. I had John sniff Gabu's blanket and began tracking after her.

The city is filled with scent traces. The smell of human bodies, their food, their cigarettes, their exhaust fumes and their effluent...In the city, no matter how astute the dog's nose, he may not succeed in tracking down his target. And I knew anyway police dogs are trained to track humans. In fact they're usually trained to ignore other dogs as they track.

John did his best for me, though.

He trotted six hundred meters from my apartment without hesitating. He looked straight ahead. He was focused on the task.

But the search ended at the intersection. The scent trail seemed to vanish there. John hesitated. He turned around once, then again, and then just wandered around for a little while.

Then he sat down and barked into the sky as if to protest. There was frustration in the growl. It may sound funny to you, but he was a professional.

John had to accept his failure. Nothing could be harder on a tracking dog than failing his search. He shared my disappointment.

If Gabu had been hit by a vehicle here at the intersection, I would have known by now.

But here her scent vanished.

So she hadn't been hit. She had been taken.

But why would anyone want to steal a fat, lazy basset hound?

As much as I adored her, she wasn't what you'd call a unanimously popular breed. It takes an effort to appreciate how cute bassets are. She was low and heavy. She wasn't the kind of adorable dog that immediately inspired kids to hug her.

Only a connoisseur, or someone jaded like me, would appreciate Gabu. Or was I completely out of touch? There are fads for breeds—akitas, Siberian huskies, shih tzus. But bassets? No, that line of reasoning was a little far-fetched.

Then why in the world would someone want to kidnap Gabu? Even to lift her off the ground takes an effort.

Motive. I'm a cop. I'd put my own training to it.

I began my investigations.

— 2 —

I'm not all that popular. At the same time, I hardly ever meet someone I like. In that sense, my life is balanced out.

She's one of the few exceptions. "She," meaning the woman who trains our police dogs. Her name is Yasutaka. I referred to her as "she"…was it all right for me to just call her Yasutaka? Yes, it was.

Yasutaka is a man's name, and she was masculine. In her late thirties, maybe. Tall and thin with strap-like muscles. She speaks gruffly, her voice crackling.

If she's a gender anomaly, it only means she defies stereotypes. You could say the same about her career.

Yasutaka specialized in animal behavioral science at the academy. Yet she worked now as a police dog trainer…You don't see the contrast? It was she who told me the two fields were diametrically opposed, oil and water.

Yasutaka said, "I'm sure you've heard of the brilliant horse who could do sums and read the alphabet. It was a long time ago in Germany. He was called *Kluge Hans*, Clever Hans. Hans would tap out numbers with his hoof, or choose letters with his nose to compose words.

"He became famous. Linguists, philosophers, and psychologists from all over flocked to his stable, to test the intelligence of Clever Hans. They barraged the horse with tests.

"Some thought his owner had set up a fraud. But Hans answered almost as well when it was someone else who asked the question. Hans truly seemed amazing. And there was no trick.

"They were so concerned with deception it took fifteen years for someone to realize what mattered wasn't who asked the question, but whether the questioner knew the answer. Or if Hans could see the person ask.

"If either one wasn't the case, Hans never knew the answer.

"The phenomenon became labeled *ideomotor reaction*. Hans had never answered any questions. Instead he had watched whoever asked as he began to tap his hoof or move his nose to the letters…The questioner, any questioner, would always themselves answer the question inadvertently—through a sudden tensing of posture, a tweak of the brow, even a shift in their breathing. Hans could detect all these subtle movements.

"This is called the 'Clever Hans Fallacy' in animal behavior studies. It was just a case of an animal picking up on human body language, yet for years some of the world's smartest people interpreted it to mean the animal understood words and symbols. It's taught as a lesson against the pitfalls in applying human standards to animals. They don't have human intelligence.

"They don't have human love.

"Behaviorists are antagonistic towards animal trainers for this reason. They can't stand how trainers ascribe animals with human traits, calling them 'smart' or 'stubborn.' They find that kind of talk intolerable. Anthropomorphizing the animal.

"But that's absurd.

"Hans interpreted a human's subtleties in a way that is practically impossible for human beings themselves. Give me a break—how is that not intelligence? Worse, they claim it's not love.

"They should know better, always trying to prove a negative.

"People who own pets know better than they. How unique each animal is. How intelligent and loving.

"See, they know."

WELL, I HAD ONLY COME to return John to her, but we ended up having this extended conversation.

She's queer in her insistence on undermining distinctions in being and thinking. She has an identity and a consciousness that runs contrary.

Come to think of it, that might be why we got along. After all, I was a cyborg—a machine in the shape of a human. Also: a human in the shape of a machine.

— 3 —

I intended to find Gabu no matter what. I had thought Yasutaka might give me some ideas with her expertise.

But my approach had a serious flaw. The scope of distinguished trainers wasn't limited to the animal. They were, by nature, experts on "love." I had come to discuss how I could find my missing dog, but the conversation ended up revolving around the topic in quotation.

Talking about love doesn't suit me well.

But the same question concerning the capacity for love in animals could be applied to cyborgs. How could love be generated in an e-brain, which merely consists of a series of switch relay logic gates? Was my perception of Motoko and Gabu based on love, or was it merely generated from some algorithm? I couldn't stop myself from wondering. It wasn't abstract philosophy.

It was practical. Because I wanted to know what drew Gabu to me.

So I asked her:

"I'm a cyborg. My body is synthetic. Half my e-brain is a crystal structure, and the remaining half is imitation neural tissue, artificially grown. My skin is sensitive; it feels. But it's still fake. I have no natural scent…"

I felt desperate, seeking Yasutaka's advice. Something inside me was beginning to break.

"…They say that dogs are almost a hundred thousand times more sensitive to smell than humans are. But what did I smell like to Gabu? Like a machine? Then was Gabu drawn to the machine in me? My brain? My brain got reformatted…Is that why Gabu left me? But I still don't understand what I lost in that…"

There was nothing more I could say at the moment.

In the pause, Yasutaka looked out the window. Whatever she was looking for, it wasn't there. It was just the sprawling, gray suburban landscape of the academy.

She finally claimed it might have been the soul.

"Soul…" I looked at her.

I hadn't expected this at all.

Does a cyborg have a "soul"? A cyborg's sense of self was virtual, a projection created within the e-brain's crystal structure. I knew exactly how my self worked. How could there be a soul there?

"Dogs…dogs have souls. Anyone who's really looked after one knows that. Don't tell me you actually believe that nonsense about humans being the only ones with souls. The dog wasn't drawn to your smell. She was drawn to your soul."

"My e-brain was reformatted," I said slowly. "My soul vanished for the moment. So you're saying Gabu went to look for it."

"I think so."

I laughed. "You don't seriously believe that cyborgs have a soul."

But I stopped laughing as soon as she said she did.

"If Gabu trusted you, and really took to you, then yes, it means you also have a soul. It has to work both ways. Yes, I believe you have a soul. Why should I doubt that?"

Yasutaka stared at me and said all this.

— 4 —

She said that a cyborg has a soul just as much as a dog has one.

—*If Gabu trusted you, and really took to you, then yes, it means you also have a soul.*

—*You also…*

—*Even I…*

—*have a soul.*

A *SOUL?*

Anyone who becomes a cyborg is presumed to have a *ghost*. It's said that the ghost from the old flesh body remains within the cyborg.

Then what exactly is a ghost? Well. No one has been able to come up with a definition that isn't circular. The existence of the ghost is something postulated, in order to implement cyborgification in the first place—the transfer of an individual human consciousness into a machine housing.

It was there, and now it's here, so it must be. The ghost.

Have you ever heard of a boid? It's a kind of program, a computer model of how animals may move in groups. The classic example is a flock of birds—hence "boid."

Each boid is given simple rules for steering. There may be hundreds or thousands, but they perceive and react only to those closest to them. Yet the entire group flies as a flock, just as birds do in nature...

Some engineer tried to explain to me the use of the boid model to describe the ghost—that the ghost is a form of negative feedback, a complex pattern that emerges from simplicity...that consciousness is a flock of birds.

THAT EXPLANATION WAS of no help whatsoever.

Furthermore, was the "soul" Yasutaka mentioned actually any different from the "ghost"? Were they different words for the same thing? If not, then how did they differ?

I didn't believe Yasutaka. Cyborgs probably didn't have a soul. The word just sounded so unlikely.

If a cyborg really had a soul, then I think he would cry. But cyborgs don't. And if they did, they would only be tears of a standard grade.

And me, this cyborg that wasn't supposed to cry, is...

...here again...

Back here again.

Here.

At the intersection where Gabu went away. Making a pilgrimage to four corners, knowing I should face a certain way, not knowing which.

With my sealed eyes I search and see nothing with them.

THE ROAD HERE is four lanes. The intersection itself is run down, ridden with potholes from the cross traffic. This is a liminal zone between downtown and the suburbs. Because the mainland slums are nearby, hardly any cars actually pass by. Even the traffic signals look cancerous...

But there's a radiance besides. Here the light flashes down from the distant, towering steeple.

The color of putty, it soars up making its own monument. The battle building is visible, in fact, no matter where you are in the city. No one here who saw it will ever forget the terror attack that made the ruin, the blast and its red blaze...

At the top of the steeple, wires hang off both sides like wings. Sometimes from this top it emits an incredibly bright blue pulse, as if singing out. As if shrieking. It's been almost ten years since the building was destroyed, but nothing has been able to end this terminal illumination.

So the flash would for a time light up the crossroads. But the roads were still abandoned.

Where did Gabu disappear to? I had no idea and no way of finding out. And yet I just couldn't seem to give up. I kept coming back here, as you will to a place irrationally, seeing if something that was lost has yet returned.

One day I looked into one of the alleys. I called after Gabu. I asked the sparse passers-by if they'd seen a basset hound. Of course, Gabu was not in the alley, nor was there anyone who'd seen a basset hound.

I was acting like a fool. The situation had gotten to me now very badly.

But that same night was different. That night was a different story...

— 5 —

I saw the blue flash come down on the shadow of a tank.

Yes, a tank, passing through the intersection. A type 101 turretless tank, to be exact. Equipped with a 120mm gun and massing forty tons. Just a bit under two meters high, it was built for stealth.

Low Observability is the somewhat hedging term. Yet it could indeed evade many forms of detection, a remarkable achievement for an armored vehicle. It has anti-radar and anti-magnetic coatings, and active thermal and acoustic chameleon transducers. The camouflage, also active, combined with the flat profile, would allow it to hide from the human observer as well as the electronic.

The type 101 is for anti-urban guerilla warfare. It excelled in ambush attacks. Its crew capacity is four, but a single person could both pilot and attack. I'm not a tank otaku. I just looked it up on the Internet. An e-brain can come in handy in moments such as this.

But it couldn't tell me why a tank was driving here through the city at this time of night. Maybe it was returning to a base. Or perhaps serving as a transport vehicle…something not trusted to go by truck.

The lightning from the steeple again flashed and cast its shadow of wings upon the pavement. The tank rolled somewhere within its cold gray feathers. It felt really ominous. The feeling didn't go away with the fading flash.

Now the tank was about to cross the empty intersection, as if it were traversing a no man's land. It completely ignored the traffic lights, of course. It didn't look the part to pay them mind.

I said nothing and watched it from the shoulder of the road.

So I found a tank, instead of Gabu. Of course, that didn't matter either. It still didn't mean anything to me…

I was staring at it with my mouth wide open, like the big idiot I am. I'm a sizeable machine, but this was a behemoth. Tanks are incredibly intimidating. Whether you're human or cyborg, you'll gawk the same.

The wheels in its treads had a hypnotic effect. True to its description, the vibrations were minute, but I just listened all the closer. I waited for the sound to fade away as it passed on…

And then it stopped in the middle of the intersection.

It became even quieter. The sudden vacuum pierced my ears. The tank's engine continued rumbling at the bottom of its silence.

Is something wrong?

Well, I had to wonder.

But that was only for a split second. The thought was torn apart by another sound, coming through the engine noise. *That sound.* A dog whimpering.

The blue flash showed me the low shape on the ground… maybe. Maybe, maybe not. My chest tightened up and I moaned.

"Gabu…?"

The basset hound whimpered again. But it wasn't Gabu. I could tell. It wasn't Gabu's voice. I felt something shrink within me, at this unexpected form of bitterness.

Gabu, Gabu, I rocked the name back and forth inside.

But only for a few moments. I could see where the dog was crouched. Right before the tank, less than three meters from the point it stopped.

I was sure it was terrified. Gabu would have been. It must have looked like a monster.

Someone had to rescue him.

Me? Forget about it. That wasn't my job. I'm not that eccentric, to scoop strange dogs away from mystery tanks. And anyway all the tank would have to do was swerve around him.

"*Sancho!*"

Someone had just yelled it. It had to be the dog's name. That same someone now ran urgently into view.

"Sancho! Sancho…!"

The stranger was hardly graceful. His run was made of sways and stumbles. An old man, not in good health, and filthy. A homeless man.

"Sancho…"

He leapt upon the dog and hugged him. Then he desperately tried to pull Sancho away from the tank.

Desperation doesn't always lead to the most informed decisions. It seemed the homeless guy was Sancho's owner. But if the owner loses his cool, the dog will often end up being even more scared than before. Now he doesn't know what to think. Sure enough, Sancho refused to budge. Again, Gabu would have been the same. The basset isn't necessarily the brightest breed on the block.

Still, this stubborn, foolish dog would have eventually moved away on his own, if you just gave him a few minutes. Dogs are always rational, even when they take their sweet time being so. The tank crew merely had to wait him out.

But the tank began to vibrate. Its caterpillar treads began to grind. It crept forward just a bit.

Just a bit. Probably less than twenty centimeters. It was a twitch. But its intention was clear.

To threaten. It was unbelievable. A stealth tank, capable of subduing a small army, announced its potential against an old homeless man and his dog.

The tank crept forward once again. Sancho whimpered, frightened. The man hugged him closely and screamed, something woeful. The tank had no reaction to either of them. Their fear bounced off the armor, as so many things in this world would.

It had to be just a threat. It wouldn't possibly run over a dog and an old man, would it? But even the threat was unpleasant. What was the point of this display? It was psychotically brutal. It was sadistic.

Something sparked inside me. Something akin to anger, something uncontrollable...

And, not under control, I had to intervene.

No, I didn't. How did I have to? I held myself back.

Hey, wait. Hold on a second here.

But I didn't wait. I was already moving forward.

That's right.

I wouldn't want you to look up to me. I'm no hero. I really despise easy heroism—or insanely difficult heroism, in this case.

I was already regretting my actions, and I hadn't even done them yet.

What am I going to do?

It was a stupid question, but it fit the moment. Because there was nothing I could possibly do.

I've been known to take out tanks before. Just me and several rounds from a massive, shoulder-fired cannon. But not just me. Forty tons of steel, the webpage said. Sure, pal. You'll open this thing up like a tin of sardines with your whiskey.

I didn't have so much as a pistol. I walked toward the tank in regret—not so much for my life, maybe, but my stupidity.

The tank was equipped with a pair of searchlights. They traversed until both locked upon my motion and pinned me down. They knew right where I was now.

I felt like a rabbit in open season. Two-fisted action against a 120mm gun. The matchup didn't look good.

A twelve-colored hologram danced on the front right corner of the vehicle. It looked like a centerfold girl about ten centimeters tall. Its naked virtual breasts bobbed up and down. Proudly, or given the circumstances, I should say, fiercely.

Breast Tank

—read the ornate glowing letters beneath the mascot. Instead of milk tank. The situation had become even more tasteless.

I drew myself up in front of Breast Tank. Then I shouted, and as nicely as possible, for them to stop.

"There's no point in scaring an old man and his dog!"

They heard me. It had an omni-directional microphone. The crew of the good ship Breast Tank couldn't have missed it.

But they made no response, other than to switch off the dancing hologram. I found her pink breasts left an afterimage. I had been trying to stare them down.

Breast Tank was still. It glowered without mercy beneath the cancerous signal light.

Well, so far, so good. As opposed to answering from the 12.7mm machine gun which, never mind the tank's main piece, could shred me without further comment. I thought about it just then because it had happened to rotate around until I was staring straight down its muzzle.

I found I had exhausted my stock of remarks.

I was trembling inside. I felt less like a big man and more like a glass ornament. All I had to do now was shatter and panic to provoke these people into blasting away.

I felt the stare of the gunman through armor plate. He frankly itched to pull the trigger.

When it came right down, I wasn't all that different from the basset. You know, there are some dogs who would have leapt right up on that thing with a growl. But I didn't have the courage to give it all I had. And yet I had already been reckless enough to confront it in this half-assed way. Surely this was worse than doing nothing.

All I could say for myself is that I must have still believed this was nothing more than a sick joke.

Did I think this was a way of offering penance to Gabu? Yes, of course. I couldn't find one basset hound, so I'd act like I was saving another.

Penance?

The unspoken thought glanced off the tank and hit me.

Penance for what? Not for not finding her.

I wasn't fully aware of the guilt I felt towards Gabu. Deep down inside I never believed I was innocent. Maybe that was why she fled. But I don't know…

What I'm really guilty of.

Maybe I'm pretending I don't know that somehow I didn't return her love for me.

I am an expert in consciousness, but love is something too abstract to grasp.

Yasutaka claimed cyborgs have souls. But you know, I don't agree with her. A cyborg doesn't have a soul, it only has a ghost. And a ghost is simply a ghost, and if it houses love, then it's only the ghost of love. As much as I might try and think about it.

My e-brain was reformatted. Gabu must have perceived how weak my love was, emaciated, like a scarecrow in his tattered clothes. I had only a starved, closed loop of feeling to offer. It was something too meager in the bowl to be called love. And that was why she abandoned me.

And that was why I was guilty.

In my grief I momentarily forgot even a tank, even a gun. My head drooped before it.

I deserved the stare of its contempt.

In that moment, all my cheap love merited was a hot quick handful of lead, like the slugs dropped down a coin slot to deceive the workings within.

— 7 —

It was precisely then that something unexpected occurred.

The helpless old man who had been hugging his basset

hound, waiting for death, suddenly arose. In considerable anger. His unshaven face trembled as he roared like a prophet.

"Sinners! What the hell are you doing?"

Then he grabbed my shoulder and pulled me away. I was too dazed to even hold my ground. It was pathetic how an old man could do that to me, but given my state...

...Next thing I knew, the old man had taken up my position. Now he was the one standing before the tank.

"You think you're mighty," he shook and screamed, *"riding upon a tank like that."*

Then he threw himself right at it. Then he balled up his fists and began to pummel it. Not once or twice, but over and over again, as hard as he could. His anger was explosive.

There was no superhuman power in the man. I saw the blood begin to spurt from between his thin-fleshed fingers. Soon he'd start to break the bones.

"Damn you...you bastards..."

He cared nothing for his state. He kept on hitting. And I couldn't stand to see it anymore.

I tried to wrench him away, wild in his rage. He screamed again, *"You bastards, you think you're so mighty, riding in this tank."*

I couldn't stand to see his broken life. The tank was nothing.

It had just happened to be the next thing in it to come along.

Even a lout like Breast Tank wasn't immune to this display. There's a limit to everything, even to armor that can stop hypersonic shells.

The heavy machine gun tilted just a bit, to adjust for the height of the old man. Now it was aimed at his heart.

Was this their pity?

My neck stiffened at his helplessness, at mine. If that gun let fly there would be no neat holes. It would blow him limb from limb.

But the homeless man couldn't have cared less. He kept on swinging. He at least gave everything he had, though it was nothing. His anger seemed almost holy. No threats could stop him. Nor the words of an idiot.

"Old man, I'm afraid you're in bad company," I said. "I think that's enough for today…" I tried to grab him from behind, but he just as quickly slipped my grasp.

Maybe the Breast Tank took pity upon me instead.

It began to rumble, raising a cloud of dust behind it. The searchlights cut away from the two of us, out to each side.

The treads went into reverse on the macadam, crushing it down like a booze bottle. It backed up just a little. And then moved forward again, around me, the old man, and the dog. It went on its way again into the night.

The tank's twin headlights formed an X over its shadow as it departed. A gesture of twin hands crossed in surrender.

The old man howled to the smoggy moon in victory and Sancho joined in time.

WHAT ABOUT ME?

Having, despite everything, a more stable life, I was too skeptical to join them in their revels. The danger past— what the hell had been up with that *tank?*

As I said, I don't figure myself the Hollywood hero. If something like that shows up at a city intersection, my inclinations as a cop are more to find out where it came from instead of taking it on. Real people—and in this situation, a cyborg should get to count—don't have the assist of CG or wire-fu. The special effects department would have their hands full just accounting for all my scattered pieces.

Motoko took on a tank. Before I pounded it with that cannon, she had already lost eight-tenths of her own body. No, not even her.

The more realistic course of action, of course, was to identify the tank and get my superior in Section 9 to lean hard on whatever unit those yahoos were from. This net search would take a few seconds longer than simply identifying the tank's model, but...

...But nothing. There was no type 101 affiliated with any local base.

So, if I just understood correctly, a forty-ton tank had come out of nowhere and then vanished into the evening air.

Independent trucking, sure. But an independent *tank?* Even with those lax fuel economy rules, no.

But something else bothered me. The scene had ended up so bizarre that I had forgot this suspicion: that the tank had been after me in the first place. Maybe the old man and the basset had been only a chance encounter that confused them away from their mission.

That was being egoistical. I'm an agent of Section 9—not a big fish. And as I said before, it was easily overkill. A sniper would have done the job, and more subtly.

But I did feel the crew's eyes upon me. They felt almost zealous, and maniacal. This wasn't a delusion on my part.

But then why...?

— 8 —

The blue flash came again, and the signals which had seemed to stop resumed.

Cars and people began appearing at the intersection as if some spell had been broken. No, even this run-down cross-roads could never have been deserted, even at this time of night.

I supposed I had frozen up again at the situation, given my state—the outrageous idea of a tank crushing a dog like mine. There must have been people and traffic around me—people and traffic who had wisely turned a city dweller's blind eye towards a tank and its prey. Fixed on the moment, it had been only my impression that the intersection was abandoned.

And once the tank disappeared, its normal traffic came back into my world. I was going to join the flow, too, and leave this place behind.

After all, I was here for Gabu, but there was nothing for me here.

The trail had ended. I had to find a different approach—whatever that could be.

As I pondered this, someone addressed me from behind.

"Thanks. You saved me."

It was that old homeless man. He was standing with Sancho on the sidewalk. His anger had subsided. In fact he wore a gentle smile.

No, I shook my head, but somehow a bit ambivalently. I realized I hadn't said anything. I added a mumble to the absent gesture. "I didn't manage to do much for you ... I was just watching you rescue your dog ... I'm the one who has to thank you ..."

"Oh."

The old man then looked at me and laughed. A dirty face, with deep dirty wrinkles. It had dignity, like a desert father.

"Tell me why you have to thank me."

"I've...got a basset, too. It's nice to see someone looking out for one."

Even though I tried to sound calm, the old man found it in my voice. He knit his brow and asked me what happened.

"She disappeared." Again, I tried, but it's not something I could say in casual tones. "So I'm looking for her."

The street philosopher seemed to ponder this. "What's the dog's name?"

"Gabu."

"As in the angel Gabriel?"

"That's right."

"I see. So you really loved this Gabu."

"I think I did." I tried to sound even more casual, but I failed worse. The tinge of bitterness gleamed in my mouth, like black oil.

"What do you mean, 'I think I did'? You're the only one who knows."

"Well, I don't know. If I really did, then Gabu wouldn't have left me like that."

"That can't be. They say dogs are man's best friend."

"But that doesn't mean the reverse. Besides, I'm a—"

Not a man. He could probably see that, and why would I bring it up? I didn't want to wallow in self-pity. I couldn't afford to. My self was all I had now.

A certain type of endorphin trickles into the brain in love. Inside the e-brain, drug-free, all such chemicals are simulated by another science, that of mathematics, spiraling up from their equation into something very much resembling all those emotions I see. You can't help but wonder, if you're a cyborg.

I had always thought my love for Gabu was sufficient, was generous. But it was virtual.

If that was true, then I'll always be a system, a consequence of these equations. How much of myself am I? What am I?

I don't get to decide these questions. They reduced me to silence.

The old man squatted down and wrapped his arms around Sancho. Sancho snuggled up to the dirty bum as he stroked his head. The man cocked up his own and addressed me once again.

"Besides," he asked carefully, "...what?"

"Nothing."

A nothing. Just because I didn't know what to say. I didn't know what I was supposed to say.

So I asked him something obvious instead.

"Did you name him Sancho from *Quixote*?"

The old man looked at me for a moment. Then he nodded and replied, "That's right."

"What made you give him that name?"

"Because I am that man. The man of La Mancha. I am Don Quixote." The old man chuckled, but there was something sad in it. "I live in a fantasy. I don't live in this squalid place. I could never survive here. I live in a fantasy world, where I search."

"Search for what?"

"For the phantasmic giant I must fight. The imaginary windmill I must tilt against."

For a moment, the old man did look noble. His filthy face glowed with pride as he spoke of his illusory attack against illusions.

Then he moaned suddenly, taking several steps back to gawk. He had realized.

Not that I was a cyborg…something besides that. I didn't think he was the kind of man to be startled at what I was.

Now he averted his eyes, trying to figure out what next to say. When he spoke, it was with discretion in each word.

"I heard that pet dogs have been vanishing lately. They say that dogs with caring owners have been vanishing without a trace. We're not talking about a dozen dogs disappearing. Hundreds. Have you heard anything about this?"

I nodded. As a matter of fact I had.

But as far as I was concerned it was an urban myth. The police are swamped these days with violent crimes against people. No one had even been keeping data on reports about these dogs. And dog theft wasn't a priority to proceed against on hunches either.

The homeless man continued with his whispered analysis. "One theory I heard is that some large organization is stealing these dogs. Maybe your basset hound, too. It's possible, don't you think?"

"Yes." Anything was possible. And having nothing to go on, there was nothing to rule out.

"Okay, then. Let's say they did. Why would they? Why would they take your dog?"

It seemed a reasonable question, but somehow I didn't get it. "What do you mean?" I stared at the old man. "I don't understand what you mean by that…"

"Why go through the trouble of kidnapping people's pet dogs? You could round up strays. Buy them for cash. You could even import them in bulk from the mainland. Why go after certain ones, of this breed and that?"

"You think there's some reason behind this?"

"Yeah," said the street philosopher, "I do."

I said nothing.

"Nothing's been proven, you understand. It's only a rumor. But one explanation I heard is that they take only dogs that are well-loved."

"Well-loved...," I repeated.

I felt my chest tighten up. Which is, of course, a simulation of a human emotional response. All of a sudden I didn't want to pursue this, not any further.

But the old man kept talking. "When I was young they used to say, 'android.' What is it now...?"

"Gynoid."

"That's right. Gynoid." The old man nodded with satisfaction. He spoke as one with authority. "I heard that the e-brain of gynoids required affect in order to make them more human. With their automatic nerve and endocrine systems, humans can respond and adjust to their environment.

"But without affect neither emotion nor intelligence can be formed. The e-brain responds not only to the environment but also—let's see—that's right, it needs an inner mechanism for affect. But how is that accomplished?"

"..."

"They say parameters which simulate the polypeptide endorphin are programmed into the gynoid brain; this is the basis in turn of a simulated adrenergic system--disinhibition of the dopamine pathways; dopamine, a catecholamine hormone, being a precursor also to adrenalin and noradrenalin..."

"..."

"In addition to these hormone parameters, there are

twenty types of endocrine model sensors. These twenty self-preservation evaluation functions serve also as parameters. So this system is installed within the gynoid's e-brain…but, I heard, the implementation of affect proved incomplete."

"…"

"No matter how the parameters are set, they still wouldn't generate real affect, of course. And it was perceived as artificial, a drawback to sales. The manufacturers agonized over the problem until they hit upon an idea. What they finally turned to was…"

I finally got a word out.

"…Dogs."

— 10 —

The old man nodded at my erudition. "That's right. Dogs. Dogs are very emotional animals. In terms of love, they're far more articulate than humans."

I was back to not replying. I couldn't afford to say anything more…

"Dogs are more loving, and more jealous, than any human. It is technically quite feasible to incorporate a dog's brain into a neural network. This would allow the emergence of a genuine psyche structure in a gynoid."

Still nothing.

"Do you understand what I'm getting at, my friend? Your dog was probably kidnapped by a syndicate and sold off to a gynoid factory."

Still nothing.

"So in answer to your doubts, yes, you really did love Gabu. Now wouldn't you agree?"

I heard Gabu bark. That's what I thought. It wasn't her. It couldn't be. It was Sancho of course.

Sancho had barked into the distance for some reason. I knew it was him. But I decided it was Gabu barking. Gabu was calling for me. That is what I decided to believe. She wished that I would find her.

The old man had listened to Sancho, and then whispered again. "Gabu likely lost track of your soul, because your e-brain was reformatted. It disappeared at an intersection, like an accident. It had nothing to do with your not loving her."

I wasn't sure I had ever told this homeless man about my e-brain being reformatted.

"You." My voice, full of awe. "Who are you?"

"Me. I'm just an old man. Nothing more, and nothing less."

He smiled at what that meant. I didn't know.

I resorted to changing the subject again, having encountered a lot of futility lately. "Right. To recap, you say hundreds of pet dogs are being kidnapped for the sake of gynoids."

"It's just a theory. I can't really say," the old man replied calmly. "But if I could give you some advice: keep searching for her."

The message window popped up in my head again.

This time the sender was unexpected. It was from the hospital. The young man, Ando…

Ando had apparently left the hospital this morning without being discharged. "Where did he go?" I asked.

"Well…" The clerk wasn't so much cold-hearted as she didn't care one way or the other. "I don't really know."

Their calling me was a formality. I was listed as Ando's emergency contact. They weren't even saying I had to actually come by.

"What would you like to do, sir? We can e-mail you the necessary documents…"

I hesitated for a moment.

I had never pledged to be his guardian. Yes, I said I'd pay for his hospital bill, but he was a grown man. What more could I possibly owe him?

Had I not remembered Ando's words then I would have left it at that. I am cold-hearted. So cold responses suit me fine. But instead I remembered. *I can't take alms from an anonymous person. Right now, I'm down on my luck, but someday I'll be back on my feet again. Then I'm going to return your favor.*

Something stirred inside me. It felt like regret. And, like futility, I'd had far too much of it anyway.

"I'm heading over there now," I told her.

I closed the window. That was when I realized the old man, too, had vanished, together with his Sancho. I looked down the four ways, but they were nowhere in sight.

The flash, the pale blue, and the echo of his voice. Except he said something else.

Take my advice. You should look for your phantasmic giant, too. You should find your imaginary windmill…

I felt only loss. There was, after all, nothing else left to feel.

CHAPTER THREE

AND TOUCHED THE
SOUND OF SILENCE

I was walking in the park with my dream son—the impossible one who vanishes, when I awaken from my impossible dreams. I was well aware of that…

He and I were headed to the university hospital. I held his hand.

The long-winded name of the *Department of Biomedical Engineering* was etched below my dream, like a burned-in subtitle, a sentence scraped into monitor glass.

"You'll vanish once I wake up. I'll forget about you," I told my son. "But I don't want you to disappear. I don't want to forget you. So…"

I stopped speaking. So what? My words hung in the air. Suddenly I forgot what I was trying to say.

My eyes wandered over the park, now immersed in the colors of fall. The maple trees were red, the maidenhair trees yellow. The autumn light upon them was soft and intense. Their leaves looked transparent in the sun, their veins visible, as they are upon the human eye.

At the feet of the trees the fallen leaves were dancing, leaving their piles to whirl in the air.

It didn't feel cold.

"So I decided to have your existence written into my memory buffer. That way you'll never vanish from me. I'll never forget you."

I lost Motoko and Gabu. I was thinking how I really didn't want to lose him too. But I knew I wasn't supposed to tell him that. I knew I wasn't supposed to tell anyone.

"People make things called neurotransmitters, chemicals in their brain. But a cyborg doesn't. It's all numerical data. You know that, right?"

My son nodded. He tugged my hand slightly.

"One of these chemicals is called endorphin. Endorphins bond with the *mu*-receptors in the brain and spinal cord—the same receptors that bind with morphine, heroin, and methadone...anyway, they're neurotransmitters. They can send 'happiness.'

"I have the data for endorphin in my e-brain. I'm planning on having it activated every time I remember you."

"Why," my son spoke for the first time, "do you have to do this?"

"Because I want to feel happy, of course. I want to feel happy when I remember you." I squeezed his hand.

He saw the error.

"Daddy, you wrote me into your memory. And then you run the endorphin routine whenever you remember me. It makes you happy. But you could be happy that way without me. You could program it all whether I'm real or not. If that's true, then how can you say I exist, Dad?"

I stopped speaking again. Then, I thought to say that he would—in my thoughts. In my wish to preserve him...

"You exist."

There was no reply. I kept on walking, waiting for his reply. As we walked, I realized I had let go of his hand. Again, I knew, when the warmth had vanished...

"——."

I called out his name.

I was sure I had called out his name, but when I awoke I couldn't recall what it was.

My last imaginary act was to turn around and look back for

him. I saw nothing, not even the trees. Only their fallen leaves now, blowing around, blowing out, fading into consciousness.

I remember thinking as I awoke, my son's become a dry leaf.

— 2 —

...It felt vaguely familiar.

But in fact I had no memory of it. Who was *this* boy? Did he resemble the son in my dreams? In some unknown way he did—but then again he didn't.

The son in my dreams, the son who vanishes. The missing son, my son.

This boy was lying on a bed with white sheets and covers. The boy's face was whiter still. His eyes were closed, and that made it oddly difficult to tell his age. In his late teens, maybe.

He had the beautiful face of a girl. It was pale and delicate, and on the verge of being shattered.

Was he asleep? His face seemed too stiff; there was none of the relaxation of slumber. He almost looked like a doll. One already broken and discarded.

The resolution on this memory wasn't fine enough to confirm, but it did resemble a hospital room. I couldn't tell where, or read his chart...I couldn't see how serious this boy's condition was...

THE IMAGE OF THE BOY was a residual visual memory found in the prosthetic portion of Ando's brain. It had been copied to a hard drive for psychiatric evaluation.

There wasn't much wrong with him—physically.

The doctors told me Ando suffered from a dissociative disorder that made it exceedingly hard for him to lead a normal life. That's how he had ended up on the streets.

He was constantly plagued by flashbacks. He would experience in the present a sensation from the past—the same sound, the same smell, the same color—and it would trigger a trauma linked to that past, so that to him, it was happening again now.

To treat him, they'd like to know what the trauma was. But interviewing Ando was of no use.

Eventually they realized in the course of monitoring his attacks that the memory of the boy emerged every time Ando dissociated. This wasn't the key—but it was the only clue. The image, and Ando's feelings towards it…

Ando had a guilt, a very deep guilt, towards the sleeping boy. One psychiatrist of an expressionist turn was of the opinion that the guilt was the real trigger of the attacks, not the sensations—that the guilt simply wished to write itself upon the windows, whenever Ando tried to steal a glance outside his mind…

That was why, perhaps, this vision looked unclear. Modern memory programs are impressive. They come with a full suite of filters to sharpen, adjust, and equalize. But they couldn't correct for a subjective state of grief. Remorse smeared the lens like tallow.

I don't think people can keep reality as it truly is inside them. Perhaps there's no such thing as a memory that is objective. If so, then we return to the practical question.

How far is it removed from reality?

Ando had been staring at the boy. Not evenly. The human eye is always moving. But minute movements that aren't registered throughout the day are accurately recorded into one's visual memory. Unfortunately so. Played back in someone else's head, they lack the cognitive adjustments that evened them out for the original witness. In this case, it only made the image harder to discern. It was as if these were the twitchings of guilt...

Ando had disappeared from the hospital, leaving only this memory behind. No one knew where he was. He didn't tell anyone.

This sadness served as a forwarding address, but then, it was where he came from, too. A man without a home necessarily lives inside his head.

I made a copy of it for myself, loading it from my e-brain into my visual field, trying to bring some sense of reality to it by putting it where reality should be.

The artificial mind comes with a standard date and time stamp feature, like a camcorder. But they weren't present in Ando's case.

There were no leads there, then, in finding out who or where the boy he remembered was.

But that wasn't really the heart of the problem, was it?

Because I still had no idea who Ando himself was.

An asinine question to myself: *Ando, who are you? And where did you vanish to?*

Of course, I got no answer. I was acting out a one-man show. As always. But this time I felt such grief, such grief of my own, that it overpowered me. And I had no answer for that either.

It was true I had no idea who this young man Ando really was. But that was true of so many people that I've met. It had begun as another brief encounter, only one out of the many. By nature they are forgotten once they pass. Why, then, remorse, for a man I hardly knew—that's what I couldn't understand.

I played the memory, until it became a memory of its own. Guilt triggered this, made me want to look without understanding. I wanted to dissociate my own self, making the imaginary cut again and again because I didn't know how to express it otherwise.

— 3 —

I wasn't supposed to kill that memory. I wasn't supposed to kill him. And yet I ended up killing him. I ended up forgetting. It was a memory I wasn't supposed to lose. But I ended up losing it...

And as I played it, I slowly came back to myself. My cop self. The memory was a fake.

It was the job of the psychiatrists who had viewed it to feel empathy towards his grief, but to not themselves feel it. I had, and gradually I found myself moving through the grief, like a membrane.

The grief was compelling to see, and intoxicating to walk within. But on the other side I could perceive that this boy in the bed was a composite of thousands of images: retrieved, retouched, highlighted, fabricated.

What Ando said after he had saved my life remained from my own memory—the low, monotonous litany of guilt.

Him most likely meant that boy. I could surmise that easily enough. The issue was why it kept on coming back as a traumatic, dissociative flashback. The trauma defined Ando; the boy defined the trauma.

And whether the boy was fake or not, the image existed inside Ando's head. And so Ando existed.

I wasn't supposed to kill that memory. I wasn't supposed to kill him.

It couldn't possibly have actually happened. In fact, I found now that beyond what my forensics told me, I also wanted to believe it was just a metaphor for something else, an image that he had for some reason embraced.

I wanted to believe that of the image—but I wasn't sure. Not at all.

The stupid self-dialogue again. *Ando, who is this boy? What did you do to him? Why do you feel this way?*

I wanted to know. But I knew I was better off not knowing. Some things—some people—are better left alone.

There are histories that shouldn't be recalled.

Like Ando's.

I'll probably never see him again.

I saw my own solitude, too, but I was sure of it. I knew I shouldn't see him again, and I was certain that I wouldn't.

It was nothing—would be nothing—new for me.

I was wrong, of course, but I hadn't yet seen my mistake.

THE REPLAY OF the memory froze with another incoming message. Togusa, again.

My partner's face filled the pop-up window. "Your ride's been fixed. Who was that guy, anyway? Pretty strange looking."

"What are you talking about?" I asked him.

"The car guy. The shrimp."

"Oh, him." I nodded. "He's no one special."

Togusa was probably referring to Ando. I assumed he'd found a trace of my experience in the car's memory. I never told him about Ando. He must have looked shady to Togusa. It was only natural.

Well, since I hadn't told him, I had only myself to blame. But I still didn't want to tell him.

I changed the subject. "My car's ready? Is that why you went out of your way to contact me?"

"No…"

"Another gynoid attack? Was someone murdered?"

"That's not it either," he indulged me. "Word is, next time that happens, we'll both be getting our dispatch orders. You won't need me to tell you."

"Then what is it?" I was getting impatient.

"You got a call," Togusa chuckled. "The *frog* wants to speak with you."

— 4 —

Have you ever wondered how dogs see the world? You can know. Just take the 13 Metro line from the city center into old town and get off at Electric Rabbit Street. Its official name is Do Greyhounds Dream of Electric Rabbits? Street, but presumably the guy painting the subway signs didn't believe it.

On Electric Rabbit street is the dog track run by Cherry Brothers, Inc. With a 2.8 hectare field, it's enormous—the third largest race park in the world, after Vegas and Macao.

The dog races here follow classical tradition. Punters purchase their betting slips at the window. They can only view the race from the paddock or on the odds display monitor where they choose their top seed. This is how it was done thirty, forty years ago.

You can wager win, place, show, trifecta, superfecta. The rules are identical to the old style. And needless to say, as in the old style, they race greyhounds (I pictured for a moment the bettor's riot a basset would provoke).

The stand even has one of those VIP rooms on the third

floor, with a lavish interior overlooking the track. The owner, Cherry Lin, greets his guests there. All in all, a far cry from the impersonality of Internet gambling.

Of course, there are some differences. Nothing can ever remain quite as it was. There are differences. Huge differences.

Greyhounds are not a new breed. They are found on the walls of Egyptian tombs. They were hunting dogs for man dating back to prehistory. Even their cyborgization is in a sense an old phenomenon. In medieval England, only noblemen could own greyhounds. In the Renaissance, Queen Elizabeth I laid down the rules for the pursuit of hares. It was fitting that the First World War, which shattered the old aristocratic world, was prefigured by a wonder seen in 1912—the invention of the electric rabbit, to be chased by hounds not through a forest, but in a loop on a closed circuit. Virtuality.

A bit of a stretch, you'll say. But let me tell you this. The new millennium dog doesn't even chase an electric rabbit. He chases only his dream of one.

The audience stares at the giant AuroraVision screens placed all along the stadium. If you need to see what's really going on, don't bother with the dogs or the field. The action is elsewhere.

The screen displays the sight of the rabbit as a wave front, localized at a point on the track. Point? The dimensions of a point are zero—how should you measure this imaginary zero?

As it translates into odds and payoffs, of course. The image is in their heads, and so the rabbit runs, until the imaginary point leads them past the arbitrary line.

The TV screens bring a bit of honesty into the process. Through computer graphics, you see reality as it seems inside the greyhounds' heads. A crowded starbow of sight traces ahead, a bright fugitive spark at its center.

It can make you a little sad, if you don't have a little money on it.

It made me a little mad for its arrogance.

We cyborgs can switch our e-brain modes easily. We know illusory lives as wide as worlds. We are constantly aware of them.

But a dog is not a student of consciousness. And these dogs had been made to have the whole world compressed into a phantom zero, chasing not the rabbit, but the rabbit hole.

...I DIDN'T COME HERE for this. I'm prone to chase my own illusions. And honesty for me means I don't even get to accept a payoff.

Froggy wanted to talk. He wanted to meet in the café bar at the dog track.

Froggy and I were acquaintances, but we weren't friends. I mean, that would be a little difficult. I'm a police officer. He's an assassin.

He was more like a star in nemesis, a dim object with whose orbit I would often intersect. We might not kill each other today or tomorrow, but there was no reason why we wouldn't the day after that.

As long as we worked different sides of the same track we'd find ourselves at a place like this from time to time to exchange information. It was like a fly meeting shit. Nothing more natural, you'll say. Except the fly still hates the stink and the shit can't stand the buzzing.

Lawman or killer, there's no free ticket out of the maze of this floating world. There's always a little give. And a little take.

That's how adults live—if not reality, then at least realistically.

Whether you're willing to compromise yourself on your way through is another story. Whether you're willing to accept the offer of an unwound thread.

$$- 5 -$$

Froggy was sitting at the bar, and when he rose it was without a sound. He got up as if his seat were a wafer. His topcoat brushed against the floor like the sweep of a black flag. Heralding the approach of a very bad man.

Greed is a funny thing. The punters sipping their drinks, watching the screens in the café, had all this time managed to chatter about the race with high nervousness, doing their best to make him their unseen antipode to the fascinating hole on the TV.

But Froggy getting up was more than any ordinary bettor could be expected to bear. With silvery clinks and glassy tinkles their cups and shots were left behind, clutching only their wagers as the place emptied out. The speed of it never failed to impress me.

The bartender used his ten seconds of reserve courage to fill two mugs of beer and dash nuts into a wooden saucer before he himself vanished. No, we weren't terribly popular in a joint like this. But what are you going to do.

EMPTY OR NOT, Froggy walked around and checked the premises. Ever the professional.

He kicked off the conversation.

"Say, you've heard of this terrorist called the Breeder, right? Don't tell me someone from Section 9 wouldn't know—"

His voice was horrible, hoarse when it wasn't squealing. Broken fingernails raking the eardrum. Even for a cyborg it managed to grate.

Froggy is officially known as Cherry Lin's bodyguard. Unofficially, he's Cherry Lin's hit man. With Lin's preventive views towards the world, it often amounted to the same thing.

His hits easily reach double digits, but Froggy's only twenty-six. He's a prodigy in other ways, already having white hair and throat cancer.

You could feel a very abstract sympathy for Froggy. He was from a small war-torn Middle Eastern country, raised in a village whose principal resource was recycled tank parts. The tanks were in parts because they had been hit by shells loaded with depleted uranium. Hence Froggy's throat. Couldn't lay the white hair on it though. Radiation just makes it fall out.

His face is flat and his eyes are wide. Yet even these weren't all the things his nickname covered.

In 1912, the year of the electric rabbit, a scientist at the University of California was already taking a scalpel to cognition, cutting the cerebral cortex, septum, and amygdala from northern leopard frogs, placing them inside a wired labyrinth. The decerebrate frog remained motionless, until a fly began to move within its visual field. Then and only then did the long tongue unfurl.

In the case of Froggy it is a long arm. The target is perfectly safe until it begins to make a move. In a long-deferred revenge the frog has a sharp knife of its own. The target's throat is cut. He will fail to draw his gun. He will fail to even touch it.

My e-brain is also a descendant of that experiment. The frogs, by the way, never did escape the labyrinth.

All frogs are carnivores, did you know that?

"THE BREEDER," I SAID, staring into my mug. There should be a science for reading one's fate in beer foam. It's topologically complex, and more manly than tea leaves. "So what?"

"I want information on him."

Steeled by a sip, I looked at Froggy. "What do I get in return?"

"The same as always." Froggy tried to look casual, but he wasn't good at that. I could tell this time he wanted my help. "I'll...give you what I have on the Breeder too."

This was interesting. I said, "Maybe Section 9 has no need for any more information on the Breeder. Maybe we already have all we need."

"That's impossible," Froggy croaked. It was very close to a threat, and Froggy didn't threaten—he killed. His awful voice told me, "No one has enough information on the Breeder. Why...he's a ghost..."

Another ghost. But he was right. There wasn't an intelligence agency on the planet that knew everything there was to know about the Breeder. For example, were you elite enough to hack into the deep data vaults of Section 9, you would receive this thrill of forbidden knowledge:

> "The Breeder"
> Occupation: Terrorist
> Sex: unknown
> Appearance: unknown
> Nationality: unknown
> Age: unknown...

– 6 –

"The Breeder." I grimaced.

Froggy nodded his head. At least he didn't have the puffy chin.

"Yeah. The Breeder."

I gave a half-hearted, full-souled sigh. I stared back at the draft beer for one more hint about my future. Nothing there. Which could very well prove to be the case.

And on that note, I started talking about the Breeder.

THE GOSSIP IS INDISPUTABLE on that there is, in fact, an operative called the Breeder. But he—or, maybe, she—doesn't nurture pets or plants. The Breeder nurtures terrorism.

Nurtures it with love and care, raising, culling, and combining plots and personages from wildly different ideological and religious lines, until an unnatural creature arises, like the orchids taught to glow with the genes of a firefly.

Sometimes the Breeder is said to conduct the final operation himself. At other times, agents take charge. Sometimes the prize bloom is even put up for sale to the highest bidder, who for the money receives a conspiracy, with fuse already cut and trimmed.

The individual operation can yield cyberterrorism, sabotage, assassination, bombing, kidnapping. But that is not why the Breeder is so feared.

It has been observed for centuries that, in theory, extremism of right and left, of those who kill for the kingdom of heaven and for that of the earth, are on a deep level, indistinguishable. It was a platitude for political scientists.

But the Breeder is far beyond the crudities of united fronts and marriages of convenience. He or she alone turned theory into engineering, learned to read in fine the acid ladders that led down into the sociopath, walking through the code to splice the memes that could make a jihadist breed with a racist, a racist with an anarchist, an anarchist with a fascist, until the end result struck unrecognizably and unlooked-for from nowhere.

Monster is not the word to respect what the Breeder achieved. It is a Protean terror.

WELL, THERE WAS NOTHING much more to say after that. But Froggy still stared at me. He couldn't believe that was all I had. He sounded horrible, and horribly disappointed.

"So? That's it?"

"Yeah." I nodded. "That's it."

"That's pathetic. You'd expect more, I mean...c'mon, out of Section 9...That really all you got?"

I shrugged.

"Too bad," Froggy said.

Then I added, "One more thing."

"What's that?"

"The Breeder is after your boss. He's after Cherry Lin."

If I thought that little interrogator's tickle would provoke him, I fell flat. Froggy didn't look surprised. He just snickered. It was a spoon clanging down a sink disposal.

Of course, I wasn't particularly surprised by the news either. Cherry Lin was a big mainland crime boss. There were dozens of people who wanted him dead. Enough to take a number and wait.

"But if you pigs know that…," Froggy said, "why don't you offer him protection?"

Well, to put it bluntly, Public Security Section 9 had nothing to gain from Cherry Lin's survival. In fact, we and practically everyone else in the world would be better off if he got killed.

But sometimes it's best not to share the truth. It's not so much a question of courtesy as it is of taste.

So I gave this freakish hit man the public-servant answer. "The Breeder has countless targets in dozens of nations. We couldn't possibly provide protection for every one of them. Even when we know something about a plot, it develops through a kind of parallel distributed processing…Section 9 believes not even the Breeder can predict the order in which each operation will emerge…"

Froggy snickered again at what he thought was mere doubletalk, cradling his mug. A government worker making excuses at a two-man press conference. But even if he didn't understand, I wasn't trying to make excuses. I was just telling him how it is.

"Can't predict it, huh?" Froggy croaked. "How about I give you a pick. Put all your money on Cherry Lin."

"No can do. We can't afford to."

"That so? Y'know…sometimes you just gotta cover something even if you can't afford to!"

All right, it wasn't too bad a joke. And I was ready to laugh.

Froggy's intentions were as obvious as a going-out-of-business sale. No matter how formidable Froggy was as an assassin, he was no match against what the Breeder could devise. So he wanted to sic Section 9 on his target instead.

I asked, "You're not really talking about Cherry Lin…are you?"

"No. This is bigger than my boss."

"How big?"

"For example," Froggy replied, "I could say it was a big mack. Mister Tung. Of *Mao Mantou*."

— 7 —

Ha, ha.

I was at a private airport later on, thinking about Froggy's sophomoric slump in humor.

This airport. I'd never seen such a vulgar piece of architecture, and in this city that's saying something. Could there be a building that flaunted its owner's wealth and power as garishly as this one?

I told myself I shouldn't be so appalled at the sight of a mere corporate airstrip, no matter how eye-burning. People are bought and sold in this town every day. Blue-chip firms expect a police precinct or two for their taxes. You get hardened veterans and shiny new cyborgs on the company payroll. Some captains will throw in a few cute meter maids to brighten an office party, with the old is-that-your-car-parked-outside? routine.

It's just the logo around this place. The giant, Mao Mantou logo.

MANTOU — STEAMED BUNS. And Mao as in, well, you know. Mao Zedong.

Everybody nowadays knows Mao Mantou. I doubt there's a human being alive who hasn't had one—had a Cheese Mao, a Big Mao, or a Double Mao.

Mao Zedong was the former chairman of the Central

Committee of the Communist Party of the People's Republic of China.

Mao Mantou, however, is a fast-food chain started by a company on Nanjing Road in Shanghai. Chairman Mao's beaming, well-fed face is now a registered trademark of the beef buns that bear his name.

The fierce worldwide battle over its market share with the Golden Arches was still the stuff of recent memory. When the greasy smoke cleared, Mao Mantou #1 of Huangpu District was up to Mao Mantou #51209 of Oak Brook, Illinois, and a cease-fire was signed in the boardrooms with Mao at 60 percent among global QSRs ("Quick Service" Restaurants, as the industry prefers, just in case people stop wanting to say—not eat—"fast food"). But everyone knows the feud could erupt again at any moment. And this time there could be even greater violence.

For now, the world is at peace, and a plastic statue of Chairman Mao looks to the future from every Mao Mantou storefront, having long supplanted Col. Sanders in public affection (The Colonel and Mao were in fact almost exact contemporaries, though it is thought they never met).

His green jacket becomes red for Christmas, and on Halloween they even put on a cape and fangs. Back when he was running things by cult of personality, his image was everywhere, until he died and the Chinese remembered that to get rich was glorious. But now Mao Mantou has brought him back again, and once again young people all over the world find fervor in his quotations, which come inside every red wrapper. He has become the popular modern symbol of socialism with Chinese characteristics, i.e., capitalism. What more could Mao ask for? Serve the people.

So, no, the "M" formed by the reflectors and giant arc

lamps above the airport, the bleary plasma and argon cliché, didn't stand for McDonald's. There had, in fact, been a brief attempt early in the century to give Ronald a makeover—turn him lean, and suchlike. It didn't work. He still lost his job to Chinese outsourcing.

THE MAO MANTOU AIRPORT is on the shore of a floating island twelve kilometers offshore. The facility is huge. The airport dome (also with a giant "M") soars up thirty stories. Like a stadium, its roof retracted, and so it did now to admit the descent of a VTOL sweptback-wing spaceplane, an eight-passenger GGB23.

Red warning sirens howled at its approach. Searchlights spun to pincer it. A video screen high up inside the dome projected a hologram of it onto the landing floor.

Coolant erupted everywhere, immersing the port in steam as it met the plane's exhaust. The guidance beams cut through, a bright, whirling web.

That's how it appeared to humans. It was a somewhat different sight for me. I got an automatic signal off the air traffic control system into my e-brain.

The input stimulus to my e-brain triggered an alert to flash in my primary visual field. It informed me that the programmatic equivalent of noradrenalin would soon start up, denoting a state of caution.

"Workers must evacuate to safe area. Workers must evacuate to safe area." The workers did just as the booming P.A. told them.

The falling GGB23 looked like a locust. No, it *was* one, a giant locust on a beam of red winter wheat.

It merged with its own hologram on the floor.

It had touched down smoothly, with the talent that comes only from programming.

The sirens fell silent. The beams blinked out with the smell of ozone. My primary visual field warning vanished too.

Finally the hologram of the plane faded, leaving only the plane itself. For better or worse.

The ramp opened on the GGB23 and two support vehicles approached it.

TOGUSA AND I HAD watched the whole process in the arrivals lounge. "Mister Tung has arrived," I told Togusa, who knew. "Let's go."

"Right."

Each of us gave an instinctive pat to our guns as we walked side by side towards the landing pad.

− 8 −

We had to guard Mister Tung. That was our current assignment.

Who was Mister Tung, and why did Section 9 have to guard him? I don't have much time to explain.

We're hardly ever assigned as bodyguards. We're not needed for that, especially for corporate VIPs. Globalization has its discontents, but it also has its private security firms. We're not trained for it, either—our job is to find criminals *before* their next target comes into range.

Unfortunately, cyberterrorism, which we were informed might be a threat, *was* in our jurisdiction.

We'll have a go at the rough stuff like any rent-a-cop, of course. But our minds can go places theirs just can't.

The unofficial reason we were here was because Mister Tung might specifically be the next target of the Breeder.

MISTER TUNG MIGHT be thought a Mongolian because of the hanzi for his name. But "Tung" is only a phonetic equivalent. It's also a little joke on the word tongue.

Mister Tung is a *composer*. Not a composer of music. A composer who weighs the variations, counterpoint, and tone of Mao Mantou's menu line.

He is partially cyborgized. A raw human lacks sufficient sensitivity for all the possibilities of their own taste. In the past, there was no objective way to measure this sense. The French, for example, used to have so-called *blenders* in the tea industry, who passed down their expertise in taste from father to son, relying on intuition and patience to judge. Barbarism.

There are billions of people out there relying upon consistency in that beef bun, after all. To ensure such 21st century savoir-faire, a nanocomputer is woven into his lingual papillae. A human has only ten thousand taste buds. Mister Tung beats that by several orders of magnitude.

One's health affects one's taste. So Mister Tung's must be completely stable. Genetically engineered hepatic cells are fused into his vascular tissue so that his body's chemical balance may remain constant. They dissolve all foreign substances in the blood stream.

Then there is Mister Tung's mood, which mustn't change either. His customers can afford a limbic system (indeed it was the principal focus of Mao Mantou advertising), but Mister Tung cannot.

He selectively deletes emotions that cloud your brain and make you buy his beef buns. And so the thing inside your mouth that you call taste does not compare with the noble rot upon Mister Tung's, where decomposition becomes initiation, an alchemical wedding between saliva, dough, and meat.

You begin to see his value. In the global scheme of things, Mister Tung was worth three cabinet members any day. The long-rumored counterstrike by one of the other chains against Mao Mantou might very well come through him. And being a cyborg with one of the most advanced computers on Earth sweeping along between cheek and gum, he was prime to be hit through cyberterrorism.

I actually like this job less now that I've explained it.

SO, WE WERE WALKING towards the GGB23 to greet Mister Tung, following the support vehicles that approached it at a careful pace.

"I don't get it." Togusa sounded disengaged.

I looked at him. "What?"

"Mister Tung spends most of his time on a corporate-owned space island. They've got private quarters for him there. Then once a year he descends to earth to conduct the blend adjustments for the Mao Mantou line, right?"

"Yeah, that's what I've heard."

"I don't get it. Why?"

"What don't you get?"

"I don't get it."

"What is it you don't get?"

"I don't understand."

I sighed. Togusa was the farthest thing from stupid, but I was in my usual lecturing mood.

"Okay"—our feet echoed in the landing dome—"the brochure says it's like this. Apparently, the human palate has evolved over the centuries. It has significant variations from region to region. Even within the same country, it varies depending on locale, sex, and age. It's affected by everything from the weather to sociologic conditions.

"Each of the major franchises has to distinguish its often identical-appearing products from the competition. Yet each also desires global uniformity for the same products within the franchise, with due exceptions for local religious taboo and beloved area soft drinks. Hence the annual blend adjustment. You follow me?"

"Yeah, that sounds right."

"So what's the problem? What's there not to understand?"

"Why'd you assume I was talking about the way the guy *tastes?* I meant him living on a space island."

My pace stumbled just a tiny bit at how he had let me ramble on.

"Well, it's hard to beat for residential security. Doesn't have to worry so much about terrorists up there, right?"

"He might not have to worry 'so much,' but that doesn't rule it out. And in fact—"

"What?"

"It's sealed thirty-six thousand kilometers up in geosynchronous orbit. Closed environment. Hard to sneak into. Better than a gated compound any day."

"Right, right—"

"At the same time, though, if someone attacks your compound you can try and run for it. Terrorists have struck orbital facilities before. It's perfectly safe, in the ways it's not deadly dangerous."

" . . . "

"I'd say the ratio of pros and cons for a terrorist target residing on a space island is six to four—con to pro. Explosive decompression, anyone? I'd take my chances down here, where the air is thick and blue."

I HAD TO ADMIT Togusa had a point.

"Space island" sounds romantic—that's why they don't simply call them space stations. Mister Tung lived on the "Satellite of the Great Helmsman"—that having been one of Mao's nicknames back in the day, used only by him and eight hundred million of his closest friends. But, the freedom of microgravity aside, his living space up there couldn't have been much more than, well, an ordinary factory worker's back in Shanghai.

As Togusa said, it wasn't even a guarantor against assassination—so why would one of the world's top corporate executives put up with it?

I figured we might find out soon. We were on our way to meet Mister Tung in person, after all. Everything would fall into place.

Figures appeared at the ramp of the GGB23. The lights on its sweptback wings cut through the steam and diffused. A phalanx of a dozen Mao Mantou staff lined up to greet Mister Tung, as befit his rank.

Once we got there to provide security, Mister Tung could emerge onto the surface of our world, with its Mao Mantous considerably more countless than the stars seen in heaven.

It's just like I told Froggy. In reality neither I nor anyone could be sure the Breeder was really after Mister Tung. But even if he was, this would not be the time for him to set any plots in motion. Everything was in order.

In order? Not precisely. Unfortunately, that wasn't quite the case. Everything was about to go out of control.

− 9 −

Out of the corner of my eye…

…I saw one of the support vehicles approaching the spaceplane. I wasn't exactly ignoring it. The e-brain's sight function, in fact, can never entirely ignore anything it encounters.

To do something without being aware of it—that's precisely what a cyborg can't do. Anthrocentrism is a lingering habit. I didn't see—I *monitored*.

Raw visual information is only a whirl of random light for the e-brain. It doesn't have any meaning on its own. Each image has to be processed and highlighted in order to form a gestalt.

The edges between things, their curvature, their borders of varying degrees of light, are selected and assembled into appropriate data. If the wrong kind of information is inputted into the retinal zone, the gestalt won't form. Unlike the human retina, a cyborg's doesn't allow indeterminacies. Once in a while, this feature can work to my advantage. This was one of those times.

An oxygen nozzle from one of the support vehicles had been cinched into the side of the GGB23. There was nothing strange about that. It's routine to replenish a spaceplane with oxygen after it lands. You don't want to have to wait for it, should you require a very sudden return to orbit.

But there was something wrong with the picture I was receiving. Oxygen should be flowing through the tube at high pressure. The vibrations would carry through the thick hose, in turn agitating the air. I was able to see the minute light in infrared from this friction.

I WAS, BUT I DIDN'T. So something was wrong with this oxygen nozzle. Even the ground crew were now checking it intently…

"Togusa!" I shouted, and dove for the floor.

The nozzle hatch snapped open, uncoiling the empty tube like a jack-in-the-box. But the jester that sprang out was four assault rifles.

The crew reached in practiced unison for the guns, offered grip-first out the hatch like a bouquet of roses. They were Heckler & Koch G36Cs, beloved of the professional terrorist—now revealed as the true vocation of the ground crew.

The G36C was once an official rifle of the *Kommando Spezialkräfte*—German Special Forces. A thirty-round magazine loading the ubiquitous 5.56mm NATO shell…fine workmanship, an excellent soldier's weapon.

Terrorists liked it for additional reasons. Even the standard G36 is 90 percent carbon resin, and the rest of the parts could be swapped for ceramics until you had a weapon you could pass right through a metal detector. And the "C" is for compact. With the stock folded, as these were, you had something half a meter long, ready to spit the same rounds as an M-16…

Pardon my shop talk. Better dying through technology.

One of the terrorists had a grenade launcher on his rifle. He aimed it at the GGB23 ramp.

Togusa had drawn his pistol as he hit the deck, aiming it at the man with the launcher. I had my own sawed-off shotgun out my coat. It wasn't as elegant as my partner's Italian revolver. But as a cyborg I do tricks with it. Magic tricks.

The grenade made a whistling sound as it fired.

My retina switched to gunfight mode. I could see the very

shock waves in the air as the heat of the grenade turned into spindle shaped infrared light. Its trajectory was clear.

I tracked it like skeet, pulled the trigger, and the grenade flew into a flock of lead.

The grenade exploded with a flash. In visual light it was a shock wave; in infrared it was a tsunami. My retinal sensitivity dropped to almost zero momentarily in reaction. Otherwise it would have been burned out then and there.

And it was then and there, of course, that the Breeder's plot had been set in motion.

$$- \, 10 \, -$$

Time slowed down.

No, it doesn't do that. Not unless you're approaching the speed of light. The shell from my shotgun flew at only four hundred meters a second. It's just so fast that you can't see it.

But I can see it.

The slugs had speared the air with bubble-shaped trails of friction heat before they hit the terrorist's grenade. They disrupted the explosive pattern, spreading it in the shape of a reverse cone, which expanded like a thrown net. Its undulations spread in red and at times in yellow brown, a spectrogram of its customized charge.

I cautioned against the grenade's power. I had to know its lethal power and its reach. I had to predict it.

Cyborgs don't have the predictive powers of a human. You don't want to ask one about your investments. But ask me what's going to happen two hundred microseconds from now, and I bet I beat you to the answer. The power of my short attention span again.

Multi-tasking is a term invented by the personal computer industry. The irony is that persons who are computers actually find it very difficult. But then, try throwing your laptop at a guy with an assault rifle.

I launched my prediction engine, switching my visual and audial fields to forecast processing. I was seeing and hearing visions of the future now. Finally, after that disappointing head of beer, an oracle.

A part of me heard my partner in the present.

"BATOU!"

Togusa shouted as he rolled on the floor and fired away. He was getting off his own shots now, remarkably quick after mine despite his lack of swapping out his own parts, like I did for my high-tech self.

Look dispassionately, even on a bullet, and you will say that it merely alters the energy distribution of one's environment. But the bullet itself will insist upon its drama. I watched the faintest arc of the magnum (my eyes see that so few things in this world run truly straight) as it pierced the shockwave of the grenade. The slug discolored it in infrared, the burst much faster than the bullet but far more diffuse. Togusa's shot was slowed in passing through, but not enough for the terrorist to notice the difference when it smacked into his body with a thud.

Togusa's Meteba was loaded with notched dum-dum bullets. When they go inside you they get all gnarled up, as does your flesh and bone and organs. When it hit the terrorist it tumbled out the other side. What had been a little finger going in was a fist coming out—out with the spongy tissue of his right lung and its freshest aerated blood, bright as it ever gets.

I saw that too.

The man fell to the ground. He was probably dead. He would be better off that way. It was, after all, our job to kill him. But I am looking at it from the perspective of his job as well.

Many terrorists have artificially grown cells in their brain. Their reflexes are optimized for pulling the trigger of a gun. And although their visual field isn't equal to a cyborg's, their foveal axons can be tweaked so that they too can perceive a bullet's trajectory. You could perform the same trick with a laser pointer for a buck, but if reason were the rule you wouldn't have become a terrorist (or a cop).

That's not all. Many go in for a little detailing on the locus ceruleus, the part of the brain that triggers the fight-or-flight response. All fight, no flight—just adrenalin and noradrenalin washing within them like glory and glory and glory.

Better to die in its midst. The only compassion I would ever wish to show them is the kind Togusa did, blowing them out in their euphoria before they have the chance to kill with it. Like the hashishim, he dies having already glimpsed paradise. What kind of paradise is it?

There, anyone can purchase an AK-47 at a convenience store. Uzi submachine guns are a dime on eBay and your junk mail clanks with sample ammo. Kill just two people a year and you can write off up to 70 percent on your taxes. And Che Guevara isn't just a shroud on a T-shirt anymore. On the contrary, you will see his face, and his throne, and his book signing, and he will shake everybody's hand. If you buy two, he might even join you for a photo.

Is that mysterious enough for the smile their corpses wear?

But take the pathos of the terrorist who wakes up in the hospital a mere cripple, neither a soldier for the cause nor a glorious martyr. There are no medals pinned to his pillow, no recognition of his sacrifice. He is still here and he has to answer for himself. He cannot kill anymore, and he has no reason to survive.

I don't know if terrorists really have a cause anymore. I mean, they swear to this, or by that, but so much of their indoctrination now is chemical or surgical. It isn't that they've become Manchurian candidates—nothing so melodramatic. They're just pressed for time in our busy modern world. If you think you can seek such a thing as happiness in a pill, then why not commitment? Who ever actually finishes these manifestos, anyway? You can be a consumer of radical ideology, like anything else. And if so, you deserve convenience as much as any of your victims and their rival brands. You know the revolution or the jihad is the shortcut to paradise. Now, with cosmetic neurosurgery, you can have the shortcut to the shortcut.

AM I RIDICULING THEM? Not really. As I said, I'm just here to kill them. I'm not necessarily any better with free will than they are. Look inside my own brain. Why not? I do it all the time.

I've got a big head. The difference between them and me is that big as it is, I don't think that I can cut the whole world down to fit inside.

That, and I'm usually a better shot.

The prediction engine told me we were under control.

We were being controlled. That's what I realized in this strobe-time: this attack was a decoy.

I got off the floor and sprinted right for the smoke of the explosion. Right for the terrorists and their three guns on me. I might as well have popped cyanide, slashed my wrists, and jumped off a thirty-two story building.

I didn't blame Togusa at all for assuming I had lost my mind.

"Batou!"

His shocked voice chased after me. My actions made no sense to him.

Togusa was my partner. I might add he was irreplaceable. I should have probably explained what I was doing. But I didn't have any time, running into a ultrashort future that I could see and he couldn't.

All I could do was yell back to him, a moment in the past.

"Backup!"

CHAPTER FOUR

NEON GOD THEY MADE

Of course Togusa backed me up. He always came through in the clutch. He rolled to get a clear angle, fired, and then rolled again, and fired again.

He wasn't going to hit anyone in particular like that, but it wasn't the point of the maneuver. Instead he was just trying to keep them from hitting him—and me. Even so there was something frantic to it, as if he was trying to underscore the wild spectacle of Batou charging three terrorists armed with assault rifles bare-handed.

It might have looked a little different had I been blasting away with my sawed-off. But inexplicably I had stowed it back in my coat.

What exactly did the Section 9 protocols say about backing up your partner's suicide? I'll bet they frowned upon it.

But Togusa wasn't the kind of guy to wallow in despair. First of all, that's my job. Second of all, he must have known as he dutifully gave me cover that I always fail to follow through on my negative thoughts.

I take positive action instead.

The terrorists didn't even try to shoot me.

My assumption—and this was one of those times when it had better turn out right—was that they couldn't shoot me. That they had been ordered not to. Since we were Mister Tung's security, it might have made a bit more sense for them to have fired that first grenade at the two of us, the bodyguards, and then attacked their target without any further resistance. But they had shot straight at the spaceplane instead, selective in their attack.

Whatever programming was in their heads, it wasn't the berserker kind, then. I wondered if the one Togusa had shot felt his death was a bit of a letdown.

YES, THEY WERE FROZEN, dumbfounded. Not only was I not an authorized target, I was neither running away nor trying to counterattack. Instead I just grinned and waved my arms, looking as if I was coming to give them a great big hug. This scenario clearly hadn't been in the briefing. Under these circumstances, what *were* they allowed to do?

Terrorists two and three ran one way, terrorist four ran another.

Let me relate what the future had told me.

The prediction engine is ultrashort term. It is designed to maximize the effect of quick combat actions: Such a blow should work thus. A shot here is likely to have this result. It works knowing my capacities and habits.

It lacks a sense of the absurd, and hence had no comment on the 100 percent chance it gave that I would in no way interfere with the terrorist strike.

It was a strange oracle for a counterterrorist to receive.

Common sense had immediately suggested to me a hardware error. I ran a lightning cascade of scans and sweeps through my head. No viruses, no Trojan horses.

But when I looked into myself, I saw a faint motion behind the mirror.

I was under observation—I had been monitored for some time.

And the watcher believed he had me under control,

hence the bland remarks about future brotherhood between criminal and cop.

It is a very old strategy for assassination, to subvert the bodyguard.

I had called for backup against the terrorists, not realizing *they* were *my* backup.

The Breeder had been counting on me to kill Mister Tung.

I COULDN'T HAVE BEEN more careless.

As Lee Morgan's trumpet had played, as I met Ando...as the car ran away...I had been suspicious of the hack into my brain, and my mistakes in response that had caused the nearly fatal crash. Had Ando not saved me...And then, my struggle to save him had taken precedence over pursuing the matter further. After all, I got to live another day, and there are few signs that admit clearer interpretation than burning gas and crunching metal.

By contrast, what had really happened in those seconds was something possible only in theory.

I don't mean the crash was an illusion. A talented hacker can alter the images perceived by the digital brain. For example, to blur the appearance of someone the victim is trying to observe. A very, very talented hacker can implant entire false experiences in which the victim will believe. But to actually access an e-brain and control it—control it so that its possessor is unaware of the control, just as the defrauded memory is unaware of its own falsity—that took genius on another plane.

The Breeder was such. He hadn't hijacked the car that evening. He had hijacked me.

I KNEW FOR SURE NOW that I was dealing with him or her. I knew it.

I had to hand it to the Breeder. I could afford to be generous, for the sake of two mistakes.

The shutdown of my e-brain that led to the car running out of my control hadn't been an error in judgment on my part. It had been an error on the Breeder's part. In the end it had provided me a crime scene to examine, not a misdirection for the hack.

The second mistake regarded the Breeder's estimation of my competence.

Cyberterrorism against the ordinary net-browsing citizen—even against a cyborg like Mister Tung, relying on his bodyguards, was one thing. Against an operative for Section 9 it literally had another thing coming.

I don't take it too personally when people try to chop me out with a gun, knife, or hand-to-hand. But I take professional umbrage at attempts to monkey with the finesse in my skull. Yes, he had underestimated Batou, I said. It was time for payback. I allowed myself that hard-boiled phrase, too.

I RAN UP THE RAMP of the GGB23.

The fourth terrorist, the one who had gone off alone, was waiting inside the hatch at the top. She seemed to be under different orders, for she swung up the barrel of her gun and pointed it right at me.

That wasn't what made me stop still.

The fourth terrorist was the Major.

Motoko.

— 2 —

Was it really her, though? No, of course, it couldn't be. Motoko wasn't here anymore. She was gone now. And yet—

Her sudden appearance froze me as much as the terrorists were when I rushed them. My move—the Breeder's countermove.

And I could not respond to this, which felt like my death.

I had read once that to say goodbye is to die a little. I saw now that after the long goodbye, the balance of it awaits the sight of the angel again, when she is a stone effigy, and you know it marks the empty tomb.

"Motoko…"

She wasn't Motoko. This was the Breeder's simplest trick, giving this woman who worked for him the features of the Major. I knew that, and it made no difference.

This woman probably didn't even resemble her at all. Probably. It was all false data, morphing her face into Motoko's. I understood that logically. I understood, but as I stared at Motoko, I felt the closed loop flicker in my e-brain, chiming like ringing glass.

There is a term for that circle inside me, but it's one that only I know. Of necessity—it was called solitude. I wasn't still any longer; I trembled with loneliness.

"It's been a while," the terrorist said with Motoko's face. "How have you been, Batou?"

Yes, I nodded. I thought I was saying, "I've been good," but that was never voiced. I only uttered something like a moan. That was all.

Motoko said, "I really missed you. Where have you been? Where did you go?"

NEON GOD THEY MADE | 115

"I don't know. Probably somewhere far away…"

Motoko said, "But now we're finally back together. Just like old times, right?"

"Yeah, that's right, old times."

Motoko said, "Batou."

"Yeah."

Motoko said, "What are you doing?"

"What do you mean?"

Motoko said, "You have to accomplish your mission."

"My mission?"

Motoko said, "You have to guard Mister Tung against the terrorists. Now take me to Mister Tung."

"To Mister Tung."

Motoko said, "That's your assignment, right?

"That's right." I nodded. "I'll do that."

Of course, I couldn't do that. What kind of bodyguard would guide a terrorist to their target? I started to show Motoko the way to Mister Tung, when I felt some heat pass by me, behind and to the left. I could see the thermal trace of the bullet, fast, but not too fast to follow, like a satellite passing at dusk. I used to watch them when I was a child.

Motoko was hit in the temple. In infrared the blood came as a comet, or, perhaps, a breakup on re-entry, as the pieces of her head rained down. In the colors under sight this was a nebula, an astonishing hollow remnant. "Motoko…" I moaned again.

It wasn't Motoko. She was just a terrorist whom my partner had shot when I should have. That's who she had been.

I saw her real face. I saw Motoko's face. I couldn't decide what I saw. "Motoko, Motoko…"

I was aware that she had already fallen, but somehow I couldn't have watched it the first time. I had recorded it instead and watched the replay over and over. I have seen loved ones do likewise in the squalid security room of a grand hotel, where all the cameras meet, looking at the one that caught and time tagged her quick steps out the door. Not the last moment she was seen alive, but, far worse, the last moment in which she was remembered.

A SILHOUETTE OF A MAN stood behind this replay, thin and fluttering, like a butterfly's wing. I knew he was the one linked to my brain. My e-brain had traced him back, and this vague shadow was all it could give me.

He was faceless but familiar. It made no sense, I knew. We had met somewhere before. I was on the verge of remembering but came up against a wall.

The man without a face grimaced and shook his invisible head and said, "Come on. It's messed up."

Messed up...messed up...messed up...

The voice faded back into cyberspace.

The image by contrast vanished suddenly. I called after the Breeder, "So was this what you wanted?"

I intended to find out what the Breeder wanted.

The car computer, my e-brain, the rifle grenade, the woman with Motoko's face...it was too much. It was too strange.

Assassination wasn't the only job the Breeder hired out for. Maybe he had something else in mind.

In my mind.

She was Motoko, the stranger, Motoko again.

I wanted so badly to see her. I began to make my way into the cabin of the spaceplane, stumbling again and again, as if miming the endless sequence of her fall.

−3−

At the end of the cabin aisle:

There was a young man.

A young man—more like a boy. He was still a teenager. He was sitting in a wheelchair, backed all the way into the rear bulkhead. He looked at me.

Suddenly, Ando's point of view on the sleeping boy was reversed. I saw Ando as the sleeping boy saw him, the new image the fit of the one that I had copied from the hospital. But that one was a fraud—

—and this boy was Mister Tung.

The composer for Mao Mantou was a teenage boy. A smile gave the merest twitch upon my lips, but it twitched the same. His fierce-sounding Mongol moniker wasn't only for PR, but corporate security. On this boy's frail shoulders after all was borne the destiny of the greatest fast food franchise humankind had ever produced. Best the competition never suspected the name belonged to a kid in a wheelchair.

Now the moment I had seen him my memory of the sleeping boy had reappeared, leading in reflex to a deeper memory still: a man, crossing before me, as though seen through a windshield. I heard his voice.

I wasn't supposed to kill that memory. I wasn't supposed to kill him. And yet I ended up killing him. I ended up forgetting. It was a memory I wasn't supposed to lose. But I ended up losing it...

I mumbled Ando's words after the memory to myself, rising with each repetition until I wailed. Crazed pictures, no longer any but fractions of thoughts, consumed me.

The cracks in sanity were now sufficiently wide not to wait for it all to come apart. I could simply jump into the nearest fissure. They grew and spread down before me like black roots, showing the way to a new entropic order of the mind, an inverse to reason.

I tilted towards it when the boy shouted "Ando!"

His e-brain was in sync with mine. The boy heard Ando through me.

Motoko, in the wheelchair, her head slack on a nerveless neck.

Now it was a scream. "Ando!" His chair began to roll forward.

This was not Motoko. As before, I thought I understood this, but this time I probably didn't anymore. Some crystal broke inside my steel head, and I screamed and leveled the shotgun at the boy with Motoko's face.

I had to at least destroy this image myself.

I was about to pull the trigger, but then I hesitated. I began screaming again, because I wanted to die, and I was better off dead.

Positive to negative. Very well, then, I contradict myself. I am small, I contain binaries.

I pointed the shotgun at my throat instead.

Togusa leapt onto me from behind, using the whole weight of his body to knock me to the floor. I didn't feel that—only the tickle of his key at the base of my skull as I re-initialized.

THE GUNFIGHT HAD CEASED. The shouting had ceased. The whole tumult of the past few minutes was only a glimmer on smoke, like the sky after the last fireworks. And a face like a flag below: Motoko's. It froze in mid-wave, as if failing to say something.

It was probably just me wanting to believe she had something to say. She had nothing to say to me.

I wasn't a good partner to her. I could never be a good partner for anyone. I couldn't relate to the feelings of others, because ultimately I wasn't substantial enough to merit someone's understanding in return.

I was a shell.

My e-brain is re-initialized regularly for maintenance. But it had never been twice in a row like this. It had been wiped, perhaps, one might say, even to the point of innocence.

I didn't blame Togusa. I would have killed the boy or me—I wasn't sure which.

But before Togusa had used the key, a long memory had spooled out, like old recording tape, from the boy's e-brain to mine. As I said before of Ando, it was, without processing, just raw impressions, incoherent sights, sounds, smells, and textures.

An image built slowly, a bright limb below darkness. Below the limb, blue, green, and white. An arc, recursive. An orbit.

Mister Tung, looking down from space.

$$-4-$$

His data flowed through my mind, like new snowmelt joining a river. Still full of ice and tumbling stones.

The memories of another are like the dreams of our own.

A RED LIGHT seemed to overlap the planet below. It blinked red, then dark, red, then dark, as if to cast the Earth as a moon and a sun in eclipse.

It was an emergency decompression warning lamp, reflected in a Plexiglas portal.

This was inside a manned space module, rotating to provide a semblance of gravity. The Earth gradually drifted away from view and in the viewing port was now seen black space. Metal fragments large and small floated by.

It was dim inside. The memory was lit only by the lamp and the Earth itself.

I somehow managed to discern the fragments were from the module. There had been an accident, but the memory image alone didn't provide enough to say. The boy's consciousness came in data packets, a slowed-down film whose frames were visible.

To understand, I had to try and remember it, not just to see.

Now I heard the ring of the pressure-loss warning alarm. Its shrillness had become very faint in the thin air. A collision. Even high orbits are full of that supremely rarified form of garbage, space junk. The throwaway culture at five miles a second.

That's what had happened to Mister—the boy—Tung. Mao Mantou's composer had been on his way to their space island in a transfer vehicle when it had happened.

I wasn't supposed to kill him. And yet I ended up killing him. It was a memory I wasn't supposed to lose. But I ended up losing it...

The boy and Ando's consciousness intertwined under the lamp inside my head. A very strange thought occurred to me: this Earth, this space even, was not eternal. It too would vanish one day, like a dream, like a waking nightmare.

NEXT THING I KNEW I was standing in front of the boy. We stared at each other.

For a moment I wasn't sure whether this was real, or another memory, true or false.

He was struggling to speak, writhing in his chair. Finally he formed a sentence, "Y-y-you know ah, ah, Ando?"

His voice sounded broken, as if it had not always been like this.

And, no, I couldn't say that I really knew him.

I had an affinity for the boy, in that I sensed his own grief, his own deep holdings of guilt.

The boy wasn't really trying to listen to my answer. He had enough trouble simply speaking.

"Ando wuh, was p-part of thhhe Mao Mantou—" (the company name, at least, *en clair*) "—spuh, space team fuh, fuh, fuh…He w-was my bodyguard."

The boy's monotonous voice was hard to take, almost as painful for me as him. And yet, the more he spoke the more I felt like I was coming in contact with another shape of innocence…

"They said I, I wuh, would have d-d-died from the c-c-c-cabin pressure buh, but Ando suh, suh, saved me…He h-had t-t-t-to use eh, extreme muh, muh, measures and I c-can't remember thhhhings, I c-can't move…But ah, Ando still saved m-m-me. He buh, blamed himself and q-q-quit the team."

The boy was determined to provide the story, but his stutter, the damage to his memory…He failed to explain the situation. Still—

"Huh, huh, he and I were c-close as buh, buh, brothers. We were so close, so c-c-close…"

His eyes drooped, and the voice faded like the clacks of an old worn typewriter, the kind that you had to strike three times to make even one faint impression.

Did he really fail, though? He had succeeded in telling me what essentially occurred.

Mister Tung and Ando had been like family to each other. They encountered a serious accident together somewhere in orbit. In his attempt to rescue the boy, Ando had ended up sacrificing the boy's key brain functions. In the hospital, Ando had looked down at the boy, and decided he could not bear the consequence of it.

That's what happened between them. There had been a time, a date, an investigation, no doubt, but all these things were trivial to compare.

– 5 –

Imagine the reverse of the space module—a submarine, sealed to keep a greater pressure out. But its hull has warped and now the waters have begun to flow in.

The submarine needs to rise to the surface, but much more of this and it cannot. It is compartmentalized into bulkheads, though—a flooded chamber can be sealed off from the rest of the ship. The crew will try to evacuate the compartment, but very soon that hatch must be closed, dogged tight...and anyone on the other side will die, so the ship may live. So Ando had done with the boy's brain. Only partially cyborgized, it required oxygen that had been almost gone from the module.

The measures that Ando had taken, the rescue as the boy's mind guttered in the empty air, had, I realized, led also to his own trauma—the injury that brought him to the streets. It had led to the prosthetic grafted into his brain, and the young man saved into a wheelchair, with a tongue that could still taste but could barely speak.

The company must have decided Ando had fulfilled the essentials of the mission.

Ando had developed a different view.

Guilt is nothing unfamiliar to me. I would keep on owing and losing others until the day I died. Motoko, Gabu, Ando. My life was one long stay of execution. There were too many people I had to beg for forgiveness. Some ledgers can't be made clear. You die in a debt that cannot be repaired.

I owed Ando—and yet, he was like me, in his grief.

It was painful to see the glimmer of acumen flash across the boy's face only to be smudged out by shadow. Ando found it unbearable and ran away. But the boy insisted on forgiving him—for he needed to be forgiven.

"Wuh, wuh, where is Ando?"

"I don't know."

He pressed on from his chair. "If y-y-you see him, please t-t-tell him...tell him I wuh, want to see him. Please tell him I, I, I want t-to t-talk to him. Please tuh, tell him...thhhhat."

"All right." What else could I say? "I promise I'll tell him."

My reply made the damaged boy smile, joy on his slack features. His smile was so intimate it was unforgettable.

AND NOW, this encounter had only taken five minutes—strange enough to make me lose track of the rest of time waiting for me out there. Somehow I had let myself prematurely assume that the meticulous Breeder had given up his plan.

My judgment may have been impaired from the re-initialization, but that was no excuse for ignoring my knowledge. The Breeder excelled at reading the mind of his target—no mere figure of speech—so that he knew how to take advantage of careless moments, however brief. He was, after all, the Napoleon of subcontractors in the war on terror.

> *The Breeder has countless targets in dozens of nations. We couldn't possibly provide protection for every one of them. Even when we know something about a plot, it develops through a kind of parallel distributed processing…Section 9 believes not even the Breeder can predict the order in which each operation will emerge…*

GIVEN UP? The Breeder never gave up. He pursued his targets to their very finish. His attack had hardly ended. In fact, it hadn't even begun. I wasn't aware of his next move until it came—and when it came, I once again couldn't respond.

He really was going to kill me at this rate.

$$-6-$$

Something stood at the entrance of the cabin. I thought it was Togusa. Or maybe an employee of Mao Mantou. It was only natural. The terrorists were all dead. There were no more opponents here.

But it was *some thing.*

My professional subroutines kicked in, good old Public Safety Section 9 training. Even if I had let my guard down, my reflexes hadn't. My finger was on the trigger of the sawed-off, my retina on reticule. I was prepared to identify and kill the enemy. But I wasn't prepared for this…this absurdity.

The Mao Mantou mascot had come to get me.

THE CHAIRMAN IN LIFE SIZE, wearing his green Mao suit. His red-star cap was cocked back at a jaunty angle, so the customer could confirm the fact, too, of his perfectly rendered pattern baldness. His arm was raised towards the future, terminating in a right hand that dangled a greasy bag of buns. "We must oppose the tendency towards selfish departmentalism," he proclaimed.

Not long after Disneyland China opened in 2005, visiting government officials considered the animatronic Mr. Lincoln (who, here, I had heard, spoke with a thick Hunan accent) and began to quietly phase out the Mao's Tomb attraction on Tienanmen Square. For decades the Chairman's corpse had lain there, in a sort of fish tank filled with noble gasses. But Mao had never wanted to be preserved thus. He had ordained just a humble cremation, not unlike the ovens that bake Mao Mantou treats worldwide daily. "We are at once internationalists and patriots," the mascot intoned.

When he was alive, statues and busts of Chairman Mao were factory-produced. Why remember his words, then, with mere souvenirs in the mausoleum gift shop, when modern factories could turn out walking, talking versions by the thousands? Indeed each Mao Mantou mannequin came with a random quote generator. The other chains had tried to compete with servomotor Colonels and sensor-guided Ronalds. But Mao was no clown or reactionary officer. He had possessed a penetrating analysis still shared today with every purchase. "It is mainly because of the unorganized state of the Chinese masses that Japan dares to bully us."

That was the thing, though—Mao statues were programmed to mind the store, not wander into hangars and saunter up the ramp into a spaceplane hatch.

A smile, not its usual smile, spread over its features.

The Mao statue looked at me. No, it wasn't really looking at me. To put it more accurately, its face was designed to *appear as if it were looking* at me. The arc of its smile got wide, wider, widest.

"All our cadres, whatever their rank, are servants of the people." It offered the bag to me. "Eat Mao Mantou."

My face was now far less expressive than the thing's. My soul, if I have one, lurched at its cheerful, quizzical demeanor, the play of emotion that now rippled on its plastic face. I had seen this in gynoids—they are designed to suggest feeling—but to see it on this effigy...

...and then I saw Mao's eyes become as mournful as my dog's.

I recalled what the old man had told me.

Dogs are more loving, and more jealous, than any human. It is technically quite feasible to incorporate a dog's brain into a neural network. This would allow the emergence of a genuine psyche structure in a gynoid.

It was supposed to be disguised as Mao with his firm lips, but it was endowed too much with emotion to hide it. It failed because it had too much love. *It ended up dying.*

I howled. That was the only way I could come to my senses, and do what I had to do, which was pull the trigger.

With each blast of buckshot the Mao statue stumbled back, but the dog's brain wired inside it still had its gaze fixed upon me. It tried to wag its lost tail, shake its lost head. A pet dog can't stop loving people. It can't stop showing its affection, no matter what circumstances people can devise.

The last round knocked it out the hatch before the walking

statue did what it had intended to do inside the ship. The hull shook with the explosion, and framed in the tombstone of the door two thermal streaks joined before my eyes, an invisible cross for an unseen animal.

I DROPPED THE finished gun with a clack.

The Breeder put things together that should never be; that was his reputation. Breeder, do you think I should commend you?

No. I swear I'm going to get you.

I had to find Gabu no matter what. I had to find the kidnapped dogs. They were no longer a crime beneath notice. They were, in fact, the shortest route to the Breeder.

When I found Gabriel, I knew that I would meet him too.

That was when I realized I'd forgotten something absolutely crucial. Forgotten? No, that's not it. I was *made to forget*. That was the trap he set up in my e-brain.

I heard a voice out of memory.

Not yet. Don't access it yet.

I remembered. That rainy evening, there was a small man with Ando. Where did that man go? Why did I fail to recall him until now? How could that be?

—It couldn't be. I couldn't have forgotten a man so completely on my own. Someone had manipulated me. The Breeder had interfered and deleted that man from my e-brain.

Not yet. Don't access it yet.

Was he referring to that interference—accessing my e-brain? Then why did the Breeder take the trouble to delete the man from my memory?

Maybe because the man was the Breeder.

I just stood there.

Togusa, who had left to allow me to try and put myself together after the key, had come running back at the explosion, wondering perhaps if I had managed to take myself apart.

He asked me if I was all right.

"Yeah, I'm all right..." I nodded, which we both knew to be far from the case. "Togusa, I need you to ask for a favor."

"Favor? What's that?"

I nodded again. "I need you to find someone."

"Someone? Who?"

"I think," I said, "it's the Breeder."

$-7-$

My dear friend Yasutaka, the trainer, was always critical of animal behavioral science. She could be, as I have said, rather combative on the issue.

She'd give an example like this: a mother cat licking her newborn. The mouth is her main nurturing tool. With it she removes the sealed membrane in which each kitten emerges into the world, clearing their nose and mouth, stimulating each to take their first breath. With it she carries them around, by the scruff. And with it she eats her own expelled placenta, and she will also eat her kittens' urine and excrement—all to conceal the evidence from predators that her little children, born blind, exist.

Yasutaka would say the scientist would measure these things, would observe this behavior dispassionately, and would have nothing to say about the mother cat's love for them. From her perspective it was simply foolish.

Maybe there was some absurdity in straining to be

objective over some things. Insisting upon the behavioral evidence…

Still, perhaps Yasutaka's claim that animal behavior science was another Grand Inquisition in the name of "objectivity" was just a *little* over the top.

For thousands of years, men had lived alongside a world of animals, entering them into roles of myth, ascribing to them their own behaviors.

There was another thing that humans saw themselves in, and wrote about with elegance—the mirror.

But it was not until 1970 that humans thought to write about a mirror in which animals might recognize themselves.

A psychologist named Gordon Gallup placed a spot of odorless dye on great apes while asleep, and upon awakening placed them before a mirror—to see if in facing a mirror they would do such things as poke at it, try to get a better view—actions that would indicate they were aware that the image in the glass was, in fact, them. He argued this was evidence of the thing which humans had thought reserved to themselves—self-awareness.

Later, elephants, horses, and cetaceans were found to pass the mirror test. A sense of self—Yasutaka would have called it the soul.

The test is controversial, as well it might be. Dogs, for one, have different eyesight than our own. There are many people, too, born blind as kittens—and who stay that way because of genes, or trauma or disease *in utero*—yet they have no trouble knowing who they are, or how others feel about them. At least, no more trouble than the rest of us who see ourselves do. There are even people who come from backgrounds or cultures that lack mirrors, and have difficulty realizing its image, when encountered, is themselves.

(On wolves rather than dogs: Yasutaka believed, interestingly, that wolves had been sentimentalized back in the 1960s—as so many other things had then—by followers of Konrad Lorenz's ethological theories in animal behavior. The wolf is reducible to fixed action patterns, stimuli and response. No room for a soul.)

Cats? Cats aren't very amenable to the secular science of "animal behavior." Any animal behaviorist knows how well they cooperate with experiments. A cat would rather starve than submit to research and its gaucheries. Cats, she would say, have souls, but they're unique, to the extent that their souls revolve more around pride than love. I might note to Yasutaka that a few days after she should lose a kitten, pride will win out over love—the mother cat will be back to her normal self. That is not precisely true of our own kind.

So BY THIS RECKONING there is only an uncertain handful of species on this planet that have evolved a soul. That's why they can sympathize with each other.

That's why humans and dogs are so amicable. That's why I can love Gabu and she can love me.

BUT THAT doesn't quite explain the gift that girl Kiri has. This is a little abrupt. Let me explain.

I bring up Yasutaka because I learned of Kiri from her. Kiri is a girl with an incredible understanding of dogs, a deep intuitive connection to them. One might think it psychic (but tests determine nothing with her).

She doesn't understand every dog out there. She's not Dr. Doolittle. She only understands those dogs whose souls have conversed with human beings.

What made her gift unique wasn't only her power to tap into the soul of a well-loved dog. She could also communicate through the owner to reach a beloved dog's soul. In other words...

She could understand what Gabu felt, through me.

— 8 —

So I took Yasutaka's advice to meet Kiri and was headed downtown on the freeway, getting off at First Avenue and 22nd Street.

That's where the SPCA is located.

I parked the car in the lot and went up to the main floor. It took me a while to get through the security entrance.

Not because I'm a cyborg. The SPCA can be a little extreme. But their security system is positively fanatical. It wasn't quite the checkpoint you pass to enter Section 9, but, you know.

My own example shows that animal lovers have to watch out for themselves these days. And I've had worse pat downs from crusty old men in the supermarket. At least the SPCA's sensor suite didn't smell like liniment.

In fact, it didn't smell of anything in here. Things were gleaming and well lit, like a corporate office. You would have expected more of a kennel aspect, maybe. If Gabu had been present, she would have been troubled by how clean it was.

Actually, knowing her, she probably would have wet herself.

I drew in my breath and spoke to the receptionist.

"I was referred to your facilities by Yasutaka…from the training center…"

I don't know why I had expected suspicion. In fact, Yasutaka had taken care of everything, as she always does. I was immediately taken by an assistant to a room at the end of the hall.

"Yasutaka has informed us of your situation," she said crisply, and then, walking ahead of me, hesitated a little. "Excuse me, Officer—"

"My name is Batou."

"You are aware of our policy."

I nodded. "I was told."

"We hope we can assist you, but, as you must have been informed, I cannot guarantee we will be effective."

"Yes, I understand. Yasutaka explained the situation…"

"I knew I didn't have to bring it up…but we've had people get very upset when it didn't work out…"

The last phrase rather low, shifting her face away from me.

I could see why she was afraid of things not working out. I was a public servant, lacking in public skills. It's usually my job to scare people. Away from work, I offer the full charm of a hulking, glass-eyed, middle-aged cyborg.

Not the best candidate to make new friends. Particularly with a nine-year-old girl.

SHE WAS IN THE ROOM IN BACK, on a very large Lors gabbeh carpet, dyed with pomegranate and featuring a pattern of dogs, that the weavers believed warded off evil spirits. I winced at the thought of what Gabu might do to it, although the gigantic Doberman that sat Anubis-like above the pile seemed to be guarding the wool as much as the girl. The Doberman was intimidating. The girl was adorable.

The large room was bizarrely full of Persian rugs, each with a child and a dog: a setter on a latticed Nain, a bloodhound on a Yalameh with latch-hooked medallions, some mutt on a Ghasgai with a tree-of-life motif and madder red border. But my eyes came back to Kiri and the Doberman—or more precisely, to the intimacy this girl and the Doberman had between them. Among these children and their companions they were special. I knew it immediately.

Yet I glanced at the female assistant to confirm it was really her.

The assistant blinked and nodded. There really was no need for me to check, was there?

I had been told by Yasutaka that she was called Kiri.

Of course, that wasn't her real name. It didn't have to be her real name. She inhabited a world where real names were useless.

I looked at the assistant again for approval and then stepped out of my fear far enough to approach the little girl.

But not to say anything.

The Doberman moved. It lifted its head to appraise me. His bony shoulders tensed a little.

Will it get up? I wondered. Will it threaten me to protect her?

The Doberman was perceptive enough not to waste his time. He knew that whomever I was, I didn't mean any immediate danger. It looked away and pretended to ignore me.

It was only pretending, of course. Should I exhibit a change in attitude, so would he, and attack me mercilessly. I tried not to exaggerate my caution overmuch.

I stood in front of her.

Kiri looked up at me. Her eyes were round and her face—it wasn't exactly blank. It was too pure to describe it quite so bluntly. I was astonished and yet felt a pang at the sight of someone so completely untainted by this world.

Perhaps romanticizing mental illness came from an honest wish to put the person before the sickness, rather than the sickness before the person.

Yasutaka said Kiri had been diagnosed as catatonic from a young age. Other doctors had favored autism, or Asperger's—her disconcerting stare was symptomatic of certain cases; more so, her intense focus, as you will see below. I didn't know the answer, if indeed there was one, as such.

It so happened that the systems in my own mind were defined by the same limitations of the cognitive science that sought to define the girl. And, although we often forget this, even a very learned definition of something is not the thing itself.

McLuhan had long ago pointed out the cyborgization humans took for granted—television, an extension of the eye; the wheel, an extension of the foot. In fact physics and engineering enabled people to see farther and move faster than their unalloyed biological heritage would permit. The human brain could likewise now construct a model of itself: the e-brain, with many discrete functions superior to the tissue that had designed it. But superiority was far down the spectrum from omniscience.

So far, that from a perspective of omniscience, you would perceive no difference between myself and her.

They had tried animal therapy. The girl achieved her first contact with the outside through dogs. She learned to use language not directly with humans, but in training puppies, learning how words represent the world.

Things were going better for her now—and remember, she was still a very young girl. By the time she grew up there was no telling how far forward she might progress, as you'd wish for any child. But that wasn't all to her story. That wasn't why I had come to meet her.

Her empathy for dogs was pathological, monotropic by neurotypical standards. "Attention-tunneling," psychologists called it. Only in Kiri's case it wasn't just a tunnel, but a wormhole. Empathy for a dog elsewhere—through space and time and its owner.

I STOOD AND WONDERED how I should address her, thinking of a nice preliminary.

But she had never learned from preliminaries. I cut straight to the chase. "I had a basset hound named Gabu who disappeared. Someone told me that Gabu lost track of my soul because my e-brain was reformatted. I don't know if that's true. I don't even know if I have a soul. But I…"

"Sure." The girl interrupted my accumulated babble. Like a small bird or mighty angel flying off into the invisible sky, she quickly added, "I'll help you find your dog Gabriel."

$$-9-$$

"So this is it?" I asked.

"Yes," Kiri nodded. "Here."

We were there, but where was she?

Was that simply her personality? Was it a different thing from her mental illness? I didn't know. All I knew was that I felt something every time I heard her speak. Innocence couldn't live here in this city; perhaps that was why she didn't.

And why Gabu had gone.

Lately, I had been looking for innocence everywhere, and wishing to see it in some strange places—including myself.

"All right. Thanks. I need you to wait here," I said and got out of the car.

We were two kilometers south of the intersection where John, the police dog, had whimpered and lost the trace.

According to Kiri, Gabu was driven from that point to this location.

A backstreet by downtown standards, only two lanes wide. Giant arc lamps were lined up over the median, putting an argon fuzz upon the image of the ruined steeple far away.

There is a world of difference between illuminating a city and brightening it up. Whatever the lamps might do was scattered by the steam that rose from grilles to meet the street-lights, a tepid inferno worthy of a low-ceilinged heaven.

The shadows of pigeons, petty souls, danced gray against the vapor.

I had learned that with training, they too could pass the mirror test.

But Kiri emerged from the car and danced there also.

The neon sign of the café beyond the fog read:

GO-D-OG

She said Gabu had gone in there.

Kiri had accessed my e-brain by wearing an AI headset and said she saw Gabu through me…It was frankly all beyond my comprehension, and cyberspace is my beat. It had been like your GPS trying to sell you on a shortcut home through the sixth dimension—which was more or less how this had all started, come to think of it.

John the police dog had lost Gabu's odor. After that there was, it seemed, only a trace of soul to follow. I wondered what Forensics would make of this little girl...but then as I've said, the police assign low priority to missing dogs.

Kiri called out as I headed inside, "You must really really love Gabu."

"Yeah, I think so." I nodded.

I *think* so? Why can't I just—

"—I do love her."

Kiri's face said that she hadn't meant it as a question.

"Do you know why my name is Kiri?"

"No." I shook my head.

"Because I'm like this city."

"This city?"

"'Kiri' means fog."

I stared at her.

"A fog clears...When I reach out and hold, the cloudy feeling I have inside me clears away. And I see the sky for a little while."

She looked at me as if I should understand.

And all of a sudden, Kiri said, "Thanks."

"For what?" I didn't know how to respond to this. I didn't know what she was talking about.

"You love Gabu. So I could hold onto Gabu's soul. Now my fog is cleared away."

After a while, I managed to mutter—I hope that I managed to say—"I'm the one who has to thank you."

"I hope you meet her."

"Huh?"

"There's someone else besides Gabu in your soul. You want to meet her too."

"Someone else…"

"Don't worry. You'll meet."

I felt something stir inside me. It shook because it almost completely resembled sadness.

"Pray for me," I burst out. "Pray that I'll meet her again."

I felt ashamed.

Pray for me.

That is not something a grown man should ask of a nine-year-old girl.

I turned around and headed into the God Dog.

Kiri called behind me, once more.

"Don't worry, Batou. You'll meet her. You're that innocent."

Me.

Innocent.

— 10 —

"A basset hound? Oh, yeah. We had a dog like that come in here once," the woman at the bar replied.

She looked at me and quickly added, "I don't mean his body, though. Just his soul."

Was she serious, or was she just high?

I gave her my best cop glare, which, like the streetlights, wasn't even cutting through the haze these days.

WITHOUT HER VOLUNTEERING the fact, I could see she was only posing as a customer here. She didn't quite fit the God Dog's profile—it was, of all things, an Internet café, for those unlucky uncyborgs not yet upgraded to getting spammed straight in the head.

She might have been a prostitute, this place her pier.

The woman was in her late thirties. High cheekbones and tan skin stretched a bit too tight over them. Washed up and out, but beautiful in her prime, which you sensed could have been as late as last week. Maybe if I had time to kill, she could be a nice drinking partner, but I didn't and then again she might not. Nice drinking partners are hard to diagnose. The condition is often confused with smackhead and religious nut.

Internet cafés are starting to feel as retro as video arcades. Why can't these people just use their cell phones and be unsociable as individuals, instead of as a group?

Maybe because they offer things besides downloads at a mere terabyte a second—often inadequate to handle today's holographic pop-ups. I said they were unsocial, but they were not without feeling. In fact, you could buy all sorts of feelings here.

The smart drinks of the previous century were a brief fad indeed—no one could convince themselves for long that drinking could make you smarter. But people always trusted drink to make them sadder, angrier, happier, and lovelier. So the emortinis and psychopolitans on the bill at the God Dog hardly needed marketing. They're supposedly non-addictive and free of side effects, which is an odd claim, considering this isn't true of actual emotions.

I find it hard to believe synthetic substances that *concoct* feelings by reacting with the brain receptors couldn't have any side effects. The practice might make more sense if you got them through a doctor. But getting one's head shifted from dodgy pharmacies online is a practice that goes back two generations now. Who's going to listen to *my* advice?

Having had natural ones once, I'd tell them it's the sheer tide of emotions that underlies one's life—they wanted hydroponic emotions at four parts love and three desire, on a club soda base with just a dash of insane jealousy.

What can you seek when you're not even in charge of your feelings? They would say this is what we seek: how to take them in charge.

The moment I entered God Dog, the woman sitting at the counter asked whether I wanted to buy her heart.

"That's all you're selling?" I said.

She giggled. "I may sell my heart," she said, "but never my body."

Again, I had no time for this. "I'm looking for a lost dog. A basset hound named Gabu. She disappeared around here. Maybe you saw her."

SO SHE GAVE ME the answer I told you, but given where we were I had my doubts about her mental state.

She picked up on my suspicious look. Wrinkling her nose, she went from giggle to the snicker more suited to her age. "So you don't believe me."

I didn't say whether I believed her or not. But I did believe she took too many mood-altering drugs. Her voice withered audibly, caught alone in a sudden frost.

"When you exchange feelings like this...you start...believing in another existence." She said it somewhere between matter-of-fact and matter of opinion.

"Another existence? What do you mean?"

"That somewhere there's like this big pool of emotions. Not a pool, even. A sea. An ocean. It's so wide that you can't cross it."

"WHAT THE HELL are you talking about?"

"See, everyone's thoughts really come from the same place. It's all connected, like the ocean. You go out and swim alone, but someone you can't see is in the same water as you."

"Everyone's thoughts from the same ocean..." I mumbled that bit around. "Not just people, though. Cats and dogs, too. Everyone. So...if you can learn not to forget to feel how water is wet, you know? That's how I felt the soul of your dog on you."

The mumbling became inaudible.

"You've never felt that?"

I thought about it. Had I ever felt that way? How wonderful that would be...I sincerely *wanted* to feel that way. But no, I never felt like I was connected to others, like I was part of some ocean.

I shook my head and replied, "Never."

She slammed her palm down on the counter, anger without a drink. "Fool. That's why your dog left you."

The bartender came between us rather quickly. He moved with speed for an old man. He said something to her I didn't try to overhear.

Then, in a louder voice, he continued, "Could you go get some ice from the back?"

"Sure," she said, acquiescently.

The bartender and I watched her go. Then we looked at each other.

"Hard to believe," the bartender said, "but she was really something, way back when."

"She still is."

"Yeah, well, she was really something way back when," he repeated.

"Wish I could have met her in those days."

He chuckled. "Don't take this the wrong way, big guy. But even way back when I don't think she would have been your type."

"Is that so? Funny how things never quite work out."

The bartender nodded seriously. "No, they sure don't." Then he continued speaking in the same tone. "I heard Cherry Lin is keeping hundreds of stolen pet dogs. There's a man called Froggy. He's in charge of the operation. Maybe they took your dog away."

...Well, I was here for information. He could tell my line of work.

It wasn't like I had overlooked the idea that the Cherry Lin group might be the ones to bring a little reality to what the Man of La Mancha had said. They were big enough. They even, through their greyhound track, had one of the largest private kennel facilities in existence. If you assumed an actual plot, they were obvious.

That was the thing, though. Until kind of recently, the tip of a derelict who told me things about the endocrine system and then disappeared hadn't been the most reliable basis on which to proceed. I had thought him a somewhat unreliable informant. I mean, besides his manner, I wasn't too sure that he had actually existed.

Froggy, looking to protect his boss, had wanted to know how much I knew about the Breeder.

Cherry Lin was a killer, but he was also a dealmaker. You didn't get to be a crime boss by chopping out every last competitor—there was a bulletproof glass ceiling somewhere above middle management and those types deemed permanently entry-level. Executives tended to display the class solidarity that the proletariat had never quite made work.

So if the Breeder was coming for him, Cherry Lin might

have negotiated, offered to buy out the contract on his life in special services.

The Breeder's Mao statue had been wired with canine neuronal cells. The evidence for it had vaporized. But I knew it to be true.

What I was actually more surprised by was the fact this bartender, a pragmatic breed, was trying to snitch on a man who could have this place torched. Not with a can of gasoline after closing, either. A Cherry Lin torching involved two men with flamethrowers, one coming in the front, the other waiting outside the emergency exit.

"…Maybe you shouldn't be telling me this." Let him see I was concerned, so he'd know it was okay for him to be.

He was only vaguely irritated at that. "Look, I'm old. I don't care what they try to do to me." He paused, as if he was about to let slip a true indiscretion.

"Besides…you put up with her. Most people here just take advantage of her feelings. They don't give a damn about her."

I SET MY EYESIGHT somewhere else until I found she had returned to the stool beside me.

The bartender glanced at the woman as he leaned over to me and whispered.

"You know, what she said about feeling the dog's soul. That was probably true."

I looked at him, and then her. Then I looked at him again. I nodded and replied, "I knew that."

CHAPTER FIVE

TAKE MY ARMS

I should probably explain what I'm doing—although I warn you it makes no sense to me.

I'm back on Electric Rabbit Street, having a great day out at the dog track run by Cherry Brothers, Inc. I'm up in the big VIP lounge on the third floor, the one with the giant glass wall overlooking the sight trace screens. The glass is one-way, something I was grateful for. It spared thousands in the stadium the sight of me begging for a walk-in appointment with a gangster.

I HAD BARGED into the lounge and asked to see Cherry Lin immediately. Lin Yingtao—Cherry Lin—was one of the biggest crime bosses in the Chinese-speaking world—which was a pretty fair chunk of the world these days. In this town he wielded more power than its mayor, and you can be sure that the Mayor couldn't get a meeting with him either—unless, of course, it was absolutely necessary.

I might be an elite counterterrorist in some circles. But to Lin I was just a fancy-sounding cop. If I'd been here on Domestic Security Section 9 business, it would have been a different matter—there were a few calls my director could make that would encourage even gentlemen like these to cooperate.

But I was twisting in the wind, and Froggy and his crew of bodyguards could plainly see it.

"Let me see him." "No, you can't."—we just went around

in circles like this, until Froggy got fed up. He raised a hand and his men backed away from me. And then he stepped forward.

He was letting me know this was becoming a nuisance.

I said, "I came here because I have to see Cherry Lin."

"So…I'm asking you…why? Because…Mister Lin doesn't need…to see you at all."

His voice had the feel of fungus on your skin—roughened, reddened, flaked. Each word oozing through the cracks like serum. In fact he used a throat mike to amplify it, yet the words were still barely discernible. People made an effort, though. There was something about Froggy that encouraged attention.

WELL, I SAID TO HIM (get this)—

"I heard a rumor on the Internet that you've been kidnapping dogs all over the city. You're overseeing an entire operation."

Froggy's too-wide stare got too wider. "Dogs…you believe…some rumor on the Internet."

"Why not."

"That's…all it takes…to get a pig riled up…these days. You must have…a lot of time…on your hands."

"This isn't official." Obviously. "This is personal."

"How is it…personal?"

"I'm just looking for a dog called Gabu. She's a basset hound. I'll back off once I get my dog back."

"She's a…basset hound…" His eyes bulged. Even more. The reason for my requested meeting was clearly far beyond faux pas.

"A-a-are you…"—like Mister Tung, he was starting to

have a little trouble with the kickoff—"…out of your mind? Don't you realize who…Mister Lin is?"

I REALIZED.

Cherry Lin is someone who has had a lot of people killed. All he has to do is snap his fingers and someone's whacked. Most of the time he has others do it—people like him don't even have to fill out the work orders—but I hear he still does it himself on occasion. The example it sets is instructive both inside and outside the firm.

And here I was, showing up at his place uninvited, re-questing an impromptu dialogue with Lin. It was audacious, it was reckless—no, as Froggy insisted, the term "out of your mind" really fit the case best.

Continuing in that mad vein, I said, "I don't care. I'm going to go see Mister Lin."

He looked away for a moment, almost in embarrassment, from what it almost certainly seemed he was going to have to do to me. He was still, after all, in his social mode, the croak-ing public face of Cherry Lin, respectable businessman.

Then he flipped a switch and turned back to me, although, of course, I had never really been out of the corner of his eye. He grinned with thick wide lips. He clicked his tongue—short, in truth—and waved his index finger merrily before my face. In the singsong of a broken piano he said, "I can't… let you…see…Mister Lin."

The outline of Froggy's body seemed suddenly to melt away, replaced with a new languid grace. His arms fell to his sides as he leaned over slightly. His upset over how to deal with such rudeness was all gone, and instead he now looked wonderfully relaxed.

A subroutine simulated a chill run down my back. The

first chordates had felt this, half a billion years ago. My spine was no longer in that organic lineage, but hardened and set, an alloy. I was a modern fossil. About to become extinct.

What happened next was entirely up to me, going by the strict letter of the law. That is, as long as I stood there still for the rest of eternity—as long as I didn't make even the slightest move—Froggy wouldn't take out his knife.

If I did move, even a little finger, Froggy would slash through my ribs.

That's right. Through them.

I usually got a small chuckle out of any punks who tried to pull a shank on me. Armored cyborg or not, it's amazing how many still place their trust in cold iron. Not Froggy, though. His serene confidence comes from farther up the periodic table, for his knife is made from his childhood supplement, depleted uranium, the tank-killer honed down to just a few atoms on the edge so it's good for slashing or stabbing. Froggy looked as if he couldn't decide which.

There was euphoria in that wretched throat, like a spirit free and streaming from a well. There was imminent happiness ahead for him, a promise of quick content. "Come on…" he pleaded without mocking. "Make a move…Maybe you'll be lucky…and meet Mister Lin."

He wasn't talking to me, I realized. He was really rehearsing for the corpse. I had heard he would engage them in a lengthy monologue, considering it improper to depart until all the blood had come out.

THEN FROGGY GAVE ME a very strange look, considering the moment. It was blank. First he had been a bodyguard, then he had been intent to kill. Now he was simply distracted.

Only one thing could countermand these roles—an order from the man for whom he performed them, his boss. Cherry Lin must have been talking on his cell phone. I didn't see a phone on Froggy—a lot of people wore them as a cheek patch these days—but that didn't mean anything. A lot of people also wore them surgically implanted in their jaw.

Froggy cocked his head like a red-toothed reindeer on Christmas Eve, waiting for the dispatch orders. He seemed loyalty personified. Of course, a lot of people went around these days with surgically implanted bombs, too.

Froggy finally looked back at me and spoke, the shock managing to come through even his wreck of a voice. "Mister Lin would like to meet you."

He implied I should be on good behavior. Otherwise, I would be taught some manners. In their inimitable fashion.

$-$ 2 $-$

Needless to say, I'd never had occasion to meet Mister Lin before.

We had some vague images of him in our files—but he was no John Gotti, reveling in the public spotlight. In fact he didn't like being photographed under any circumstances. It was prudent, perhaps, considering that he had already been reported killed four times in the last decade.

A few years ago, one of the weekly men's magazines did a manga with a character supposedly based on Cherry Lin. It was a real collector's item, because it had never been collected as a graphic novel; even most of the back issues it ran in disappeared. The artist and his editor had disappeared too.

The tragic, or rather comic, thing was that the figure in

the manga hadn't resembled this man at all. The artist had depicted him as an exquisitely coiffed mafioso, chortling evilly as he commanded flunkies in a three-piece suit. But in fact, as I was led by Froggy into a kitchen behind the counter, I mistook Cherry Lin for a short-order cook.

YOU SEE GUYS like him all over Taipei. The outfit consists of a wife-beater, shorts, and apron. He swings his ladle as he yells, making fried rice and gruel, twice-cooked pork and noodle soup. He's cheerful, rude, greedy, and vulgar. That's what Cherry Lin looked like—albeit with the apron over a polo shirt and chinos. He was small, gray-haired, and thin. He appeared to be in his sixties.

He looked poor more than anything.

It'd taste good while you were eating it: 2-aminopentanedioic acid, 2-aminoglutaric acid, 1-aminopropane-1, 3-dicarboxylic acid, *simpliciter* MSG. Lin's unlikely appearance had put me in mind of the case of the taster, Mister Tung. One might think science had determined everything there was to know about taste centuries ago—the taste buds for bitter, sour, salt, and sweet—but it wasn't until the dawn of the 21st century that Feng and Zhao, among others, identified the receptors on the human tongue for a fifth taste, *xiānwèi* or *umami*—their most common trigger, the much-maligned MSG.

As with the late lesson of the mirror, we presumed we knew our senses, and were found to be ignorant. Yet what we had thought of the world came from that ignorance we had called knowledge.

It would be nice if I, too, looked like something other than what I was.

As he worked the wok, he would glance over at the AuroraVision monitor beyond the window, at the spectral chase of the hounds.

On the screen the imaginary rabbit, localized as a haloed point upon the screen, was seen as if it were real, as if it could run. To the dogs, unaware that humans were deceiving them, the rabbit *was* real. Yet the humans, who knew, focused all their attention upon the illusion…

It was not so simple. To say the TV image—or the image in the dogs' heads—was an illusion was to miss the point. The technology behind these inputs activated exactly the same places in the brain as "real" inputs would—it wasn't like you used a different kind of vision to watch a blue sky than you did a video. Likewise the simulated track of the rabbit was wired straight to the same lateral geniculate body in the dog's brain where the signals of real sight would have come.

The point was not that the image in the head or on TV was fake. The point was that for the dogs there was no rabbit to catch. Contrariwise the same illusion served a practical use for the humans: entertainment, and for some, a winning bet.

It had always been so. Even when the rabbit had been real, the dog never got it. They had been bred only to chase. In Elizabethan times the original rules of coursing had said:

> *He that comes in first to the death of the hare, takes her up and saves her from breaking, cherishes the dogs and cleanses their mouth from the wool, is judged to have the hare for his pains.*

The carny was wiser than the philosopher, who wanted to talk about the objecthood of the walnut shells. He knew truth could be found—could only be found—in the applicable knowledge of its function.

So concentrate on epistemology and avoid metaphysics like the plague.

Take my word, it's a sucker's game.

I DIDN'T TRY THESE insights on Mister Lin. I got the feeling he managed to avoid thinking himself half to death as I do. Talking others to death seemed to be more his concern. Like that short-order cook running down the menu, he just kept yakking away.

"DOGS, YOU WANT TO know about dogs, well let me tell you, Officer, it's no secret we keep several hundred greyhounds here, it's the second largest track in the world—"

In fact I knew it to be the third, but remembered Froggy's hint about manners.

"—When I say several hundred I mean it might be several thousand, that's a detail-oriented bit of information and I leave this to subordinates, I have many interests to attend to and what counts in leadership is overall vision, you may take what makes those dogs run as an example sir. We here at Cherry Brothers Ltd. might have had occasion to resort to extreme measures to possess all these greyhounds which we have, Mr. Officer, I won't deny that and in fact we take pride in the motivated posture which has made the Lin Group preeminent in so many rewarding lines of business. But I swear to you, although I realize I am not under oath and further remark that this lounge is equipped with the latest antisurveillance devices, that in all this we have done nothing illegal. If you were to ask instead whether there have been times perhaps when we nearly broke the law well then I can't deny that, this is a jungle and this is also why I retain an expert legal staff by which you will be aware the Lin Group has at every instance managed to avoid indictments of the sort regrettably common in a society which makes too frequent employ of the courts. What is to be understood is that there is a line, a certain line, Mr. Officer, which may be glimpsed, and defined, and walked along, and perhaps on occasion shifted slightly in its exact position but is not to be crossed. And besides—"

There was more? But even Cherry Lin was out of breath. I might have not been there as he added oil to his wok, sizzling and smoking. The fan above the grill turned on again automatically. So did he.

"—we are of course here at the Electric Rabbit concerned with greyhounds which we race, Mr. Officer, not basset hounds, which are lazy and eat too much, sir, in my professional opinion I don't see why anyone would want to have one. There's going to be a shift on the odds in race number six but I would still give you the tip to bet on Sir John Oldcastle out there who was just up in mid track, it would appear that the favorite Locrine got knocked back on the first turn and Thomas Lord Cromwell shuffled early."

Maybe this was the signal that although it suited Mister Lin to be polite, no part of this conversation should be construed to imply any obligation on his part to remain so. I still didn't like to hear someone making fun of my dog's breed. Gabu was in fact a glutton who had never done an honest day's work in her life—but to have it said by a mobster frying noodles somehow pushed all the wrong buttons in me.

No matter how pissed I was though, Froggy was correct—I really was better off keeping it to myself. Now that I had met Mister Lin in person, I thought more deeply on a remark I once heard about him, that he liked to carve up his enemies and serve them. I had always taken it as a sort of metaphor.

But the impression he gave of being a Taipei short order cook instead of the underworld kingpin he was remained so strong, I had the enduring wish to just speak casually with him. Also unwise. Yet I had to start responding to this blather, or I'd get nowhere.

I began speaking cautiously, as if my tongue was pressed against a knife. Which it was.

"I just don't understand why you need several thousand dogs, as you say, sir. Eight dogs run in each race. You run fifteen races per night. Even if you were to include dogs in reserve and the ones you're training, you wouldn't need more than three hundred at most."

Cherry Lin continued to stare at the race results. "Now as for The Puritan they were giving him nine to four earlier today but he was offstrided in the second and Vortigern well he made a rail effort but was pinched back. It's a matter of blood, Officer, we need blood, we need to have blood, as much blood as possible."

"Huh?" That wasn't very polite—but nor was it enough to make a man like Mister Lin pause.

"A dog is injured shall we say, it has been known to happen in our races, they are knocked about and bumped back and this is all happening at very high speeds, imagine yourself having a running mishap at seventy-two kilometers per hour. A dog is injured, it needs blood and I can assure you Mr. Officer, that there are some very concerned people in the stands as well, of course the race schedule must go on but in addition to this our customers become quite attached to many of these animals, they say dogs are man's best friend and it would be a tragedy if this injured dog were to die for want of a liter of the proper blood and they have thirteen types, did you ever know that?"

No, I had never known that. Luckily Gabu had never gotten anything more than a scratch.

"And just as with human beings the universal donor type is type O negative, there is such a universal donor in dogs. This type is referred to as DEA 1.1. negative, not the Drug Enforcement Agency, Officer, but Dog Erythrocyte Antigen, it is only a matter of circumstance, there is no link that can be materially proven, but it so happens that 60 percent of greyhounds possess this type blood. Now perhaps you've wondered about cats, well we don't race cats either but I can tell you that they have only three blood types, just three and yet none of the three are a universal donor. But does that really surprise you, Officer?"

I think I shook my head again.

"These hundreds or perhaps thousands of greyhounds to which I refer are themselves dogs which have been around the track too many times at other venues, venues that lack the humanitarian concerns of Cherry Brothers, Ltd., and at such places they would have been euthanized with a six-cylinder gasoline engine which pumps carbon monoxide into a sealed room in which they are confined giving, were the same process applied to humans, the appearance of suicide. I am digressing but to return to the greyhounds in our care you take a razor and shave a small patch off the skin of the neck and then you just stick it a little in the jugular vein, this is the preferred method and after you have taken the unit you can be assured we give them a treat containing iron for good health."

Cherry Lin took his knife and began to slice up some *qing-geng-cai*, rhythmically tapping it against the well-worn cutting board. He continued to talk as if humming along to the beat of the blade.

"So you see therefore Officer that we need a lot of dogs and for this purpose greyhounds are ideal, blood calls to blood as is the saying. For this purpose basset hounds would not be so useful. They are fat and lazy with no concern for health unlike the virtues if I may so use a word of qing-geng-cai, in this dish adding calcium, beta carotene, and Vitamin K to prevent hemorrhoids."

I kept my mouth shut again.

Look who you're dealing with. Just think about it. The prudent thing would be to accept his account and back down. There's other avenues. Yes, that would be the wise choice.

But I wasn't after wisdom, but innocence. When I thought of my dog's eyes, seeing me, really seeing me, I decided I would not back down.

"DOGS HAVE SOULS. Every single dog has a soul. It doesn't matter whether it's a greyhound, basset hound, or whatever. You know it's true. You went to town on those dogs not because you wanted their speed, or even their blood. You wanted their souls, Mister Lin."

— 3 —

Cherry Lin seemed to ignore what I had just said. He took a fistful of the qing-geng-cai and tossed it into the wok. His face wavered behind the sudden smoke. When he spoke again, his sentences were much shorter.

"Do you know why my company is called Cherry Brothers Ltd.?" he asked. "'Brothers,' but where's the other brother? I had a brother. Do you know where that brother is?"

I was confused. "No, I don't know."

"He's here." Cherry Lin pressed his finger to his temple. "Inside my head."

I could relate.

"Twenty-eight years ago I tried to come to this country with my twin brother. My brother never made it.

"We were illegal immigrants. There must have been thirty of us. We were packed into this little ship's hold. We could hardly breathe. No water, no food—we couldn't even lie down. We stood the entire time, stinking, shitting our pants—but hoping to make it across the ocean. Then it would be a new life, and what we went through to get there wouldn't matter. Like a woman in labor. You follow me?" He flicked the knife in my direction with only slight hostility.

"But we were attacked by pirates in the East China Sea. They've been in those waters for thousands of years. A big container ship, *that* they're not going to take on. But a small boat full of migrants? Easy pickings. They pointed their guns down into the hold and hauled us all up to stand on deck.

"So what they did was take everyone's savings. Everything we had on us to start over. They called out a certain price you had to meet per person—otherwise, they would kill you. My brother and I had enough money. The problem was…"

Cherry Lin took a vial of dry star anise and sprinkled it into the wok, before drenching the ingredients with chicken stock. Then he took a huge jar of chili paste under one arm, so big that he simply scooped in his ladle for a portion, and then plopped it down upon the dish. Now he began to stir with vigor, showing a skill that appeared compulsive. An appetizing aroma drifted around the room.

He seemed to have become engrossed in his cooking, having forgotten what he'd been talking about.

Or maybe this was his new way of jerking my chain.

"The problem…" I had to remind him. "What was the problem, sir?"

Cherry Lin nodded. "The problem," he repeated, "was that we only had enough money to save a single person. Not enough for us both. Before I knew what was happening, my brother jumped overboard, solving the dilemma."

Lin looked straight ahead for a moment, essentially, into nothing.

"I worked hard all my life since then for my brother's sake. Not for his memory. For him, do you understand? I wanted to get him back, no matter what. I knew it was possible. My brother and I were identical twins. We had the same genes. We were one person, together in that womb, before he split away from me. It was simple, you understand. I'm a clone like all identical twins. A clone of him, from my perspective. I don't want to copy myself. I just want my original back."

— 4 —

Cherry Lin poured some broth from the wok into a flat saucer and called for Froggy. He tasted the soup and nodded respectfully, giving his boss a thumbs-up.

Loyalty had its drawbacks for the inquiring chef, though. Lin asked him suspiciously, "Don't you think it's a little bland? Maybe it could use some salt."

Froggy insisted it was fine, it wasn't bland, but Cherry still looked skeptical. He replenished the saucer and turned to me. Now he wanted the cop to have a taste. It's not something I'm optimized for, like Mister Tung. I shook my head and Lin seemed to get the idea, but looked a little sad at it. So he tasted the broth himself and wondered aloud about fennel.

Finally he put the saucer down and went on as before.

"So I had a few clones made to try and rescue my twin brother. Chinese invented vertebrate cloning, you know, guy at Shandong University did it with a carp back in 1963. Mao didn't care; he already had all the masses he needed. Of course, cloning humans is prohibited by international law—" yes, and I noted it had been a while now since Lin had bothered to call me Officer—"so it's a little expensive, but not as expensive as learning how to apply the forced-growth techniques they use for commercial livestock to a human being. People who clone their pets get a newborn puppy or kitten to raise, but I didn't want to raise a baby brother. I wanted *my* brother back, the same age."

Mister Lin gave the wok four vigorous shakes, sounding like cymbals on a drum set.

"It takes big money to break the law on that level, very big money. Hundreds of millions. This is what I meant when I said I worked hard all my life for my brother's sake. Maybe you've noticed my own style is not the most prosperous. But I have taken care of our business very well here, for Cherry Brothers, Ltd.

"Did any of it work? No. None of it worked. The brother I remembered sparkled with life. Someone who loved life until he could love someone else's as much as his.

"But none of the clones had that. None of them were him. None of them had a soul."

He set the wok down with more gentleness than I had seen all day. "So you're exactly right…Batou, was it? What dogs have but clones don't is a soul. Well, I guess we all know about dogs. After getting nowhere for so long, I started to think about it. What is a soul, really?

"I had several hundred, or should I say several thousand dogs stolen to find that out. I subsidize a lot of research, you know, and I'm told that some of it eventually bubbles up into the journals. My PhDs have to be discreet, of course, first because they'd get life without parole, and second because I'd have them killed in prison. But there you go, Officer, my work is a benefit to society. They say the law doesn't keep up with science. That must be true, it sure as shit doesn't keep up with me."

His old confidence seemed back. Or so I thought—

"But, even motivated as these scientists are, they found that converting a dog's neuron signal patterns into a closed circuit and downloading them isn't the same thing as copying its soul. It's similar but not the same, two words which sound very much alike. You can't graft souls like they do limbs for amputees. It ends up more like those phantom limbs amputees say they feel, the ghost, as it were, of the ghost. I could show you some people today who look a lot like me, Mr. Officer, but they're nothing like my brother."

He stared straight at me, wanting to know what I was going to say next.

"Why…" I asked slowly, "did you have to steal pet dogs? As you said, money is no object. You could have bought as many as you wanted from a breeder." The last word carefully, with no hint at double meaning.

I wanted to get it out on the table, but a face like Lin's will make two fives a royal flush.

"Had to be pet dogs. Only a dog that's been loved can have a soul. A dog that's not loved might as well be in that pound, waiting for the gas."

I felt a sad tremor in the air. It appeared and then vanished.

I hesitated. What I was about to tell him was crazy. Of me. Still, I had already decided I would stake everything to find Gabu.

"You're lying. There's not a grain of truth behind that story."

I have to say what I've got to say. That's how I've lived— and that's how I'll go on living.

$$- 5 -$$

Froggy, who had relaxed somewhat in the convivial, masculine bonhomie, managed to freeze and bulge at the same time. He always dressed well—much better, I knew now, than his boss. I heard barely a whisper of fine twill as he took a step towards me.

"Stop," Cherry said quietly. His voice sounded ragged as his bodyguard's. "Don't you get it? I'm tired of doing that. I'm so tired of it."

FROGGY STOPPED.

With no outlet, the blood he had wanted to drink seemed suddenly to evaporate into air, where it still hung in the room, yet could do him no good. For the moment he had neither master nor target, confused as a child when grown-ups argue.

Cherry Lin looked at me and asked, "What did I lie about?"

There was a pause. I was hesitating. People say honesty is a virtue, but hadn't I already taken this too far? Yet if he wasn't going to say it himself—

"Your brother didn't jump into the ocean. You shoved him off the ship to survive. You killed your brother."

Now Froggy's glance snapped back to Cherry Lin in disbelief, in shock. I realized the story of the brother must have been important within the organization, one of those legends by which great leaders are defined.

"You lied about producing clones to get your brother back. Like you said, you're not detail oriented—you leave it to subordinates. You don't expose yourself. When people say you kill, or you've been killed, it wasn't you—it was them."

THE TENSION WOVE itself together with silence, stretching down like a rope trick in reverse. You could climb it from dreams into desolation.

In the room I thought of Motoko suddenly. Whenever we were together, I always felt like we were bound by this same kind of strand. I couldn't tell if it had possessed the same sadness, though. I didn't want to think that we had felt like this. Even if we had.

Cherry Lin finally spoke up, and said, strangely, "Are you saying I'm too corrupt? That I've lost all my innocence..."

"I don't know, sir. I'm only a public servant. I might

judge someone by the law, but I can't judge his soul. I have no right to."

"Really," said Lin, with flint. "Well, because as it happens this isn't even a court of law, let alone a church, I feel I can confess to you, Officer. You did judge my soul. You said there wasn't a grain of truth behind my story. That is exactly what is behind it. A grain. I still want my brother back. I want us to be as close as we used to be. That part was true. The part which was a lie was where I said I was doing it for him. I am doing it for me. I want to become an innocent man again. Considering who I am and what I have done, do you regard this as delusion on my part?"

Lin was furious, yet I knew he wasn't strong enough to hurt me. Froggy, who could, could not.

It was unfair that I should have to do this, but I needed to help him somehow.

"I don't know, sir. I don't even know what makes someone innocent."

"What makes someone innocent..." Cherry Lin muttered.

"I have a dog named Gabu, sir. She's my basset hound. I love her more than anything in this world. Just as you want to find your twin brother, I want to find Gabu. If you stand here and swear to me that no matter what actually occurred, your wish to see your brother again is for innocence, then my wish is no different.

"A *dog*, Mister Lin. Just one dog."

CHERRY'S FACE LOOKED even more haggard. His gaze seemed not to have left me, but it had in the last few moments passed through where I stood, looking somewhere far beyond, into deep waters.

He said in an incredibly low voice. "Do you know the steeple?"

"Yes."

"I'm not certain…but I believe your dog is there."

– 6 –

It looked like the fog, but it was the mist. It didn't block; it blurred. The neon glow wavered as if tinged by vacant thoughts, and retreated like a passing memory.

It was all outside the window; it was nothing outside the window. What use did I have for a view, after all? My trusty GPS and auto-drive could be counted to get me and my car there, even if the road proved to have been very roundabout.

I felt the urge to recall something. I knew it was an illusion. There was nothing I needed to recall. An empty cyborg was occupied by empty reflections upon an empty haze. That's all it came down to.

It had come down to here.

I stopped the car across the way from the steeple.

I LOOKED UP at the wires that hung down from its sides. Tonight there was distant thunder, and I thought that the lightning might call to the battle building again, as it had that day a decade ago. No, that was grotesque.

It hadn't been a force from heaven that had killed several hundred innocent people here—no matter what the bombers' web site had claimed.

I started to make my way forward.

A figure appeared in the mist.

He stood in my way.

I tensed, reaching for my sawed-off. I thought he might be the small man.

The Breeder.

"Oh, it's you," the figure said cordially.

It was Don Quixote, the homeless tank-fighter. "I thought we'd meet again," he told me. "How have you been?"

It seemed too long an answer to burden him with. I was just relieved to see a friendly face, unshaven as it might be. "I've been all right. Where's Sancho?" I would have liked to see his basset, too—at the moment.

"He's fine, just fine," the old man nodded and then smiled happily. His mouth had about three teeth left, but it had, shall we say, a simple charm. "You know with the rain and all, he's staying home. I didn't want him to get wet."

"Home?"

"The underground tunnel at the park. There's a shelter there. It's not so great, but you stay dry."

"Sure, but what are *you* doing out in this weather?"

"Well, someone's gotta bring home the bacon." The old man smiled and shook his bagful of scavenged food. Half-eaten beef buns, wrapped in the Chairman's face.

"You're very kind," I blurted out. What did that mean? Something. And then I asked him, "Tell me how I can be kind like you."

He only seemed mildly puzzled. "How? I don't know. I never really thought about it that way. He's all I got. He's all I got. Nowadays I don't want anything else…"

I stood there, getting wet, whereas he just stood there.

"What about you? Did you find your dog?"

I must have looked sad. But I didn't say yes or no—I only shrugged my head, as if to say I wasn't sure.

That seemed to be all he needed to understand. "That's okay, that's okay, friend. I know what you found. You found your phantasmic giant. You found your imaginary windmill."

"Maybe..."—I looked towards the steeple—"...I don't know."

I turned back to him, squatted down, and with a hush said, "Please tell me who you are."

"Just an old man, like I told you. You already know."

He chuckled and the mist came by to shroud him. The old man became a silhouette. And then the Man of La Mancha was gone again.

I staggered, as if I was looking for him, but I really wasn't. I wouldn't find him. He was not what I was to find.

Tell me how I can be kind like you.

I wanted to know, because he had been right about everything.

I would find out once I entered the ruins before me.

$$-7-$$

In some places the wreck of the battle building might have been cleared away long ago.

And it still might happen, if the money was right. But even before the attack, the neighborhood had struggled for redevelopment. And ever since it, there had been concerns at city hall about exactly which way the steeple was going to fall when the ruins made their final collapse. Some said this way, some said that way. Whichever way it was would determine which block exactly got smashed to pieces, and the general unspoken consensus downtown was to wait and see.

For now the place was left to the derelicts. But even the derelicts didn't go in. Too many people had died in there already. It was sensed, somehow, that no one would count a few more.

FROM THE OUTSIDE, it appeared better. The soaring walls still stood.

The inside, of course, was where the bomb had gone off. The charge in the lobby had ripped a hole ten stories tall— seven floors up, three floors down. Rubble had rained down all about the crater, through which the sub-basements below were visible. A faint whiff came from the broken sewer main at its bottom.

The bodies had been removed, of course, along with every part of them bigger than a finger. Vermin had long ago taken the rest to themselves. The stains of the victims were all that was left, a dusting of cinnamon, on the floor, the walls, the ceilings.

All around the vast lobby with its bomb-blown dome above were clumpings of concrete, rebar, and office furnishings. It was difficult to see more than a few meters to the right or left. Parts of the exterior supports had staved in here and there, exposing the steel frame in agonized knots. It was amazing it had stood for as long as this.

Water came pouring down everywhere, thin as little threads, or wide as sheets. It flowed over the heaps like a topping and gathered at their base in large puddles. Strangely, it made no sound.

THE FLASH I HAD SEEN before from a distance, off the top of the steeple, I saw now inside. It was a spark, somewhere high up in the ruin.

I had felt Gabu's presence the moment I entered the steeple. But it wasn't only her. Lots of dogs were here. It was strange I didn't hear a bark. Were they kept drugged?

The upper floors were still intact, straddling the gouged levels below like a milking stool. The elevator had been in the central core, and needless to say, there was no power—I was going by my starlight scope and what seeped in through the blown-out windows. More than adequate to find the stairs.

And the Breast Tank, squatting around the next pile of rubble.

I REMEMBERED THE antipathy I had felt before, when its gun pointed down on me, the old man, the dog. The cool contempt of a person commanding stealthed machinery, origin unknown, arriving without warning to kill.

It was a fitting ride for the Breeder.

"I've come to talk to you again," I mumbled, as I approached the Type 101.

It wasn't as vague as a premonition. There was no way a man as shrewd as Cherry Lin would sell the Breeder out completely. Lin had already decided to negotiate with him. I was just a poison pill in the strategy.

The moment I left the Electric Rabbit, Lin would have informed him that word had come to his ears a certain Section 9 officer might be snooping around the steeple. Cherry Lin had nothing to lose, whether I killed the Breeder, or the Breeder killed me. And if we both died, that would be the elusive synergy they say works out in less than 30 percent of mergers.

I already had my shotgun out and shucked. Why, I wasn't quite certain. It could make a terrible mess out of the bastard, sure, but he would have to be nice enough to unscrew that armored hatch first.

Despite our prior acquaintance I think he was about to do me no favors.

I had been saved a lot by others lately. This one was up to Officer Batou—but I still wanted someone to pray for me.

Pray for me. Pray for me, for Motoko, for Gabu...

– 8 –

Breast Tank fired without warning.

My visual field switched to battle mode the moment it began. The hot trajectories came for me, but I was no longer there. I twisted and turned to the future time of the prediction engine, dancing between the demisemiquavers of the machine gun's cyclic rate.

I got graze after graze—chips and chunks of me flailed off by the whip of the 12.7mm. At its firing speed any hit to my head or torso would mean ten hits.

But I wasn't hit. I wouldn't say I was lucky. Luck had nothing to do with it. Every millisecond of life I earned now was through hard work.

I was astoundingly fast in battle mode. You could say something about how in it, I was the ultimate fighting machine. Not really. Battles aren't won by ultimate fighting machines. They're won by very good ones that are mass-produced, like the Type 101. My custom-made cyborg body is merely what it takes to *dodge* real weapons.

Actually fighting them is out of the question.

The 12.7mm slugs broke a secondary hail off the rubble —shards of rock and plastic I was less adept at avoiding, as they came in at dozens of vectors, not just the machine gun's deadly one. I was stitched by the swarming air.

And there was, as always for me, another problem besides.

"Battle mode" is a bland name for what in your car or bike you call red-lining. I'm designed to do it. I'm not designed to do it all the time. In fact, the longest time I've ever done it was exactly 4:53.87'. This was confirmed by the technicians who had the job of rebuilding me afterwards.

I had to destroy this tank—something, of course, I knew that I could not do—within five minutes.

THE FRICTION FROM another burst left spirals of infrared in my eyes and infrasound in my ears, passing two centimeters off my chest like a locomotive. An oblivious pop-up in the corner of my perception noted that total system failure probability was now at 9.3 percent. 11.7 percent. 14.1 percent. It could happen at any moment. Five minutes was just the point of certainty.

I decided to try something stupid, and bucked my sawed-off at Breast Tank. Just to add waste to futility, I did it again and again and again and again. Boo-yaa.

I didn't quite expect the pellets to penetrate its armor. In fact I was fairly sure they would never even reach the tank. I wanted to see what would happen. Several slugs from the tank met and spattered the shot in midair. I could see the large ripple they made in the field of fire.

And I tucked myself into it and sprinted for the tank, reloading my gun all the while, in battle mode much faster than one of Mister Lin's greyhounds. I wondered what odds he had placed.

This was the aforementioned stupid thing I wished to try.

Then Breast Tank stopped firing for sixty milliseconds and in the unexpected quiet I heard the tiny baffled noises of its autoloader as it slipped a 120mm shell into the breach.

At least the Light Brigade had gotten a poem out of it.

I drew my .40 Smith & Wesson backup and aimed straight down the cannon and speed-pulled the trigger. I'm not sure whatever happened to all those little bullets down there, but a moment later the gesture got exactly what it deserved.

The sonic boom of the tank shell was ear shattering as it lanced out the pipe and ripped the air in two, gleaming with heat like a magic spear. This time it was the shell that grazed me, picking me up in passing and smacking my body to the floor. I counted this a success, still having a body.

As I rolled, the floor billowed and creped. Concrete debris and gouts of blinding dust fell around me so that I couldn't confirm this by sight, but I heard something, probably the wall, come crashing down.

After a few seconds on my back things cleared enough to note the motion of doves, scattering from their purchases at the top of the hole high above. Small-arms fire had been beneath them. But at the boom of the cannon they fled, seeing no signs of peace were needed here.

− 9 −

IT BOOMED AGAIN and the artillery heat bloomed, red-colored and voluptuous, a giant blood dahlia budding and creasing until I screamed, my eyes nearly burned blind.

My sight and hearing were now down to mere human under the onslaught. They would have to do, presumably proving just as useless as cyborg senses had been.

I kept on screaming, getting up, running away, trying to make a dash for the door.

Breast Tank dropped into gear and chased after me. This was soft—its dampened treads making no more than a hum, a cheerful song of victory.

I couldn't outrun it, even in my lingering last seconds of battle mode. Still less could I outrun the next shot from its cannon, now trained directly on my back. He could fire now, or decide to stretch the fun out just a little more.

I crisscrossed as I ran the labyrinth, like a mouse in a maze, the scholar tracking me all the while with indulgence and a 120mm gun. Around the final heap of rubble was the exit. I could no longer hear the shell being loaded into place. It wasn't necessary to hear it. I wouldn't see it, either. I wouldn't even feel it.

The exit—and before it the bomb crater.

I made a flat leap across as the Type 101 fell backwards into the pit, its one final shot tilting high above me to punch through the wall of the steeple and land, it was later determined, three kilometers away in a deserted playground.

It crashed through the first subfloor and rested there for a breath until the second too crumbled to dust and it landed at last at the very bottom, in the stink of the sewer.

BREAST TANK WAS still a moment. Then its treads began to find traction.

The Breeder was the deadliest terrorist our proud race has ever produced, his genius without cause or ideals, only a desire to refine the fear of a world already sick at heart with it. He moved the air with cryptic passes and a thousand miles away winds blew down bombings, burnings, gassings, and plagues. If he died right now he would still leave victims in legacy, from plans set in motion only he knew of. They would pile for him in tribute, in Accra and Calgary, Montevideo and Bonn, Niigata and Jaipur, for years and years like long fireworks, until every last string of the fuse played out.

Better still that he died right now.

My shotgun boomed down into the sewer, into the methane roaring blue.

MY KNEES BUCKLED at the edge and I felt my body cave, overcome with the urge to fall asleep and rest. Didn't I deserve to now?

Not yet. I wanted to free the dogs. And I had to free Gabu.

I dragged my lead feet towards the stairs. They weren't blocked by rubble. Much.

— 10 —

The dogs were kept on the ninth floor. I didn't stop to count them, but there were well over a hundred.

The entire floor was filled with dozens of clean, soundproofed cages, a tidy automatic kennel system running on concealed power lines. Food, water, gates that opened on timers for exercise runs—even little robots to scoop the poop. The SPCA itself could have hardly complained, except, of course, for the fact all of them had been kidnapped.

The Breeder had never been a kindly soul. The dogs' emotions had to be disturbed no more than their theft itself made necessary. Otherwise they would have been no use for the gynoids.

I FOUND GABRIEL in the thirty-second cage. She first stared at me blankly. Then Gabu began wagging her tail as if she suddenly realized—oh, it's him.

I said to her, "Hey, how've you been?"

It wasn't a particularly moving scene. Did I give her a big, warm hug? Nope. Did I then stroke her head? Nope, not even that.

Exposing our feelings just wasn't our cup of tea. It was somewhat out of character. We just sort of acknowledged each other. I often held her in my arms, true, but that was just because she was too damn lazy to walk.

"I bought you some Bajidu," I told her. That was my biggest display of emotion.

Gabu looked at me as if saying, oh yeah, that's nice. Plainly I didn't have it on me at the moment, so she gave a half-hearted wag of the tail. Then she yawned.

I led Gabu out of the room, who at least condescended enough to leave under her own power. Yasutaka would want to get involved helping the other dogs get back to their owners…for now, they'd be okay. I briefly pictured myself trying to lead a twenty-breed exodus down nine flights of stairs. No thanks. I'd be lucky not to have to carry Gabriel down every one of them.

Gabu and I headed for the stairwell, my limping and her pattering down the hall.

But this high place was the roost of the flash, and before we could descend it came and cast a shadow on the opposite wall.

Someone was there, in the light with wings, an angel.

"Ando…?"

Yes, it was him.

He stood with his back to the wall and his look, as when I had first rescued him, was at nothing.

THE BREEDER HAD intended me to kill Mister Tung. But every plan of his had carried alternates. And I knew well that even dead, the plan was still in motion.

He had tried to gain—he had gained—control of me. But if I failed, then whom did he lay charm on next? The body-guard who had already failed the boy most of all, who grieved for him, whom the boy still loved. It was elegant and cruel.

But I liked Ando too much to let it happen. Innocence was not so simple either. It had qualities. It was a thing of individuals.

I was a brooder, a loner, but I sensed he could use a friend. And I wanted to be him.

I called out to him again, "Ando…" I could get him specialists. I could give him back the life he thought he didn't deserve.

HIS EXPRESSION SHIFTED, indicating emptiness, a fleeting dream…

This is what Ando was looking at: not nothing, but at emptiness.

Then he said, "I wasn't supposed to kill that memory. I wasn't supposed to kill him. And yet I ended up killing him. I ended up forgetting."

He thought he was guilty. But if he was guilty of anything, it was of being too innocent.

He was guilty of nothing else, but it delighted the Breeder to have him kill in his innocence.

"Listen, it's going to be all right. We're going to go to the hospital. When we get out, Mister Tung wants to see you. He doesn't blame you, you know."

"Tung…"

"That's right. We'll get you okay, and then you'll see."

"Tung…"

"Right."

I nodded and attempted to access my e-brain's message site. It would be good to let the boy know I had at least found Ando.

But my e-brain was malfunctioning after the fight below. I got linked to my short-term memory instead. A superficial memory I should have deleted:

Who was that guy, anyway? Pretty strange looking.
What are you talking about?
The car guy. The shrimp.
Oh, him. He's no one special.

IT WAS MY CONVERSATION with Togusa. Togusa brought my car over from the repair shop. That was how he'd come across the image in the car's sensors. He saw the "strange looking" guy and "the shrimp."

I had suspected the small man was the Breeder. Now I

realized there was no reason to believe he had ever existed in the first place. After all, the Breeder could have arranged the hallucination with ease.

But Togusa saw "the shrimp" on the car's memory playback. It was Ando, tall and handsome, whom he hadn't seen.

So my hallucination had not been of the small man. My hallucination had been of Ando.

The boy Tung remembered Ando. But he had remembered Ando through me. I had already known Ando's memories recovered at the hospital were fakes…

I HAD MET A MAN. But I had never met Ando. Ando didn't exist.

But this man before me, this man now reaching out his hand to embrace me, did exist.

"Yes," he whispered, or, perhaps, sighed. At any rate, there was at least no triumph in the voice.

I felt the cold steel muzzle press against the back of my neck. I didn't have to be told the Breeder's gun was loaded with high-explosive Teflon rounds. No point in using anything less on old cyborg Batou, when the game was finally over.

And then Gabriel, of all possible angels, let out a ferocious growl and attacked the Breeder, to end the small war in this rickety heaven.

The gun in my neck veered just for a moment, and I slammed my elbow into his chin and turned and drew my .40 s&w and fired. I couldn't afford to aim. I just fired.

The Breeder screamed. Was he hit, or did he simply stumble back through the hallway window, to float amidst the shards? Why was his body never found?

In the lightning he had appeared for a moment to spread wings.

But the following darkness was absolute, and in its contrast he was not seen.

THESE WERE IMPRESSIONS that came later, along with the thought that he was twice-fallen.

And if I don't deserve to be born again, then at least I did regress for a time, crying once more as a child.

For what I hadn't had, yet lost, and for the nulls of the name I could now hear.

Ando.

EPILOGUE

It was three days later, the weekend.

I was on my way to pick up Bajidu at the convenience store again. I was buying it every other day now, ever since the projector had somehow come to change its mind. It was becoming part of my routine.

But something very strange occurred on this trip, in broad daylight.

WAS IT A COINCIDENCE? I saw the small man as I came out into the parking lot.

He was homeless, but he wore decent clothes. He was collecting empty bottles in the parking lot.

—So he exists?

I couldn't take my eyes off him. It was rude, but I could hardly help it. I felt as if I'd encountered a lost species.

He finally noticed me staring him down. It couldn't be pleasant to get this from a stranger, and from the looks of me it could also be frightening. He started to move away without making it too obvious.

BUT I SAID, "HEY!"

I didn't want us to part ways—not like this. I had to ask him something.

Well, I thought I sounded polite, but that hardly reassured him.

"The supermarket gave me permission. I'm allowed to collect these bottles," he said timidly.

"That's not it. That's not it at all. Er..."—he wasn't beginning to look set at ease—"...I apologize for making you feel uncomfortable. Sorry about that. I didn't mean to. The thing is, there was something I wanted to ask you."

"Ask me something..."

"Yeah." I nodded. An idea suddenly occurred to me. I asked him whether he would sell me a couple of his bottles, and casually held out some cash.

It wasn't much, but he seemed taken aback by the gesture. "This much..."

"Compensation for frightening you. Please...take it," I said. He took it.

Then I had to ask him.

I was still haunted by the memory of what he had said on that rainy evening, hunched over my windshield.

Don't access it, not yet.

I asked him what he'd meant by that. Access what?

The man wore a blank expression, but then he seemed to recall his words. He shook his head.

"You heard me wrong, mister. That wasn't what I said at all. I was just talking to myself. Don't act on it, not yet. I was thinking about how I wouldn't get tipped for washing a car in the rain. I had been drinking a little, you see. Otherwise I would never have tried to do it in the first place."

I STOOD IN A DAZE as he asked me whether he could go now. Without waiting for my reply, he left. I stood there with the empty bottles for quite a while.

It felt good to laugh.

A MESSAGE CAME IN from Togusa:

A gynoid's murdered its owner and two policemen. This is our eighth case. The Chief's going to activate Section 9…

By the time his dispatch was over, I wasn't laughing. The sun had set while I was standing there, and I was headed over to the crime scene.

So that was how this story came to an end. This story—

I was walking in the park again and for the last time with him. I think Gabu was with us, but I'm not sure.

Was it autumn, or spring…? I'm not even sure about that. Was the pavement covered with flowers, or with leaves?

In my dream, I was telling my son who vanished about a friend. About the one who had nearly been. I told him about the man whom I couldn't befriend in the end.

Do you think it's strange for me to have shared that with him? It felt natural, because I knew my son was like him. He would disappear, too.

Then, I felt: maybe I can't love this son, either.

The story ended with the last thing I ever said to my dream son. "I still regret how I couldn't say goodbye to my friend. I wish I could have said goodbye to him."

We walked on without exchanging a word. Then, the last thing my dream son ever said to me.

"He might not ever have existed, but your feelings for him

did. Father, people may not be there. And people who are there
will one day vanish. But your feelings won't.
"So you have to learn how you feel."
He squeezed my hand, and was gone, having not been there.

—I could feel warmth there still, sometimes when I awoke.
I'm not supposed to dream, but I want to. I remember what
it was like. It was when he shared something true with me.
That's how I feel. That's what I'd like to believe.

AFTERWORD

MASAKI YAMADA AND MAMORU OSHII

ON *INNOCENCE*

This following was a discussion held
at the Japanese premiere of the film *Ghost
in the Shell 2: Innocence* between director
Mamoru Oshii and novelist Masaki Yamada.
The moderator was Shinji Maki.

Animation director Mamoru Oshii was an aspiring writer during his student years. In fact, it was Masaki Yamada who put an end to this very aspiration. They were almost the same age (Oshii was born in 1951 and Yamada was born in 1950), but, according to Oshii, his hopes were dashed as soon as he came across the twenty-four-year-old Yamada's first work, *Godhunting*, ("Kami gari") in Japan's *SF Magazine*. Oshii ended up becoming a fan of his work, and even now claims Yamada as among his favorite writers. Yamada himself had become familiar with Oshii's work as a filmmaker, and felt an affinity to it as someone of the same generation of creators. *Ghost in the Shell 2: Innocence, After the Long Goodbye* was their collaborative project.

1. WHAT "INNOCENCE" MEANS
After the Long Goodbye *wasn't a standard*
film novelization…

YAMADA: The story precedes the narrative in the film. Oshii told me I could do what I wanted, so I didn't hold back, and went full throttle writing a hard-boiled story.

OSHII: My own hopes to become a professional writer might have been dashed when I encountered Yamada, but I could have at least done some kind of novelization of my own film (as Oshii did with *Blood: Night of the Beasts*, a novel based on his 2000 anime project *Blood The Last Vampire*—ed.). I decided not to write an *Innocence* book, though, so I was wondering who might end up doing it instead. I had no idea I would end up encountering Yamada again [*laughter*].

YAMADA: I had my own take on the title *Innocence*. In the futuristic world in which the story's set, the city is expanding infinitely with its memes, whereas humans themselves are wasting away, becoming more and more inanimate. I don't blame this alienation on science as such, but rather in humans' investment in creating the illusion of humanity. Hence the only dynamic ones in the world of *Innocence* are its dolls. Those who created them no longer have a sense of their own human identity or reality anymore, and, invested in the illusion of themselves that the dolls carry, they then become terrified of them, terrified of turning into them, frightened of their greater innocence.

OSHII: I wasn't actually the one who came up with the title *Innocence*—it was the film's producer, Toshio Suzuki (who is also the producer of Hayao Miyazaki— *ed.*). I had a different name for the film in mind. I'm too embarrassed to mention it now, though. Coming up with titles is not my forte. But I couldn't imagine any other once Suzuki contrived *Innocence*. The title, combined with the film's ending theme, "Follow Me," really sums it all up. Such names can be incredibly evocative. One of our animators insists on calling it *Ghost in the Shell 2*, but everyone ignores him [*laughter*]. (Note that Oshii's original 1995 *Ghost in the Shell* enjoyed more success outside than inside Japan. Hence his recent sequel was, in fact, called simply *Innocence* in its Japanese release, there being no particular publicity benefit to associating it with the original!—*ed.*)

I wasn't particularly conscious of the themes of purity and innocence when I first came up with the story. I mean, those themes are very remote to me. I don't know whether Suzuki had managed to figure out the underlying motif of this film, or whether my earlier suggestions had provided a catalyst, but *Innocence* somehow ended up being the most appropriate title. It was the same thing that happened with *The Angel's Egg*. (Oshii's first feature-length animated film to be based on his own original concepts, released in 1985 in Japan through Animage Video, a label, like Suzuki's Studio Ghibli, associated with publisher Tokuma Shoten—*ed.*) Suzuki even came up with the logo design for *Innocence* when he made his pitch. He knew something concrete would persuade me. I liked the word "innocence," because in this case it didn't imply "good." Yamada mentioned "purity," instead, and I absolutely agree. It refers to a state where there's no imprint.

2. IMAGINARY SOULS

*Was there a discrepancy between the world you created
in your novel and the one depicted in the film?*

YAMADA: It was almost identical. Music played a more prominent role, however, in my book. They showed me a rough cut of *Innocence* a while ago and described the story to me, so I was able to imagine the rest. I also knew that dolls and dogs would be prominent motifs, so I incorporated them into my novel.

As I said, dolls have only the illusion of humanity, but that status makes them all the more innocent. Dogs are also above humans. In the film, the soul-like entity that only exists in life forms is called a "ghost." I discussed the concept in my book, referring to it as a "soul" instead. In the novel, dogs—in fact, only pet dogs which are loved— have souls. Horses have souls, as do whales. Humans, however, don't. That's the premise of this book.

OSHII: When I went abroad for the previous film, *Ghost in the Shell*, I had to answer questions like, "What is a 'ghost'?" "Is it any different from a 'soul'?" "I thought only humans had souls."

Although I believe that the original creator of the *Ghost in the Shell* manga, Shirow Masamune, had his own ideas in mind by using the term "ghost," my use of it in the films was intended precisely to avoid the kind of debate I just described, by saying "ghost," instead of the much-freighted term "soul."

The soul is like a UFO. Only people who need one will see one. So pondering whether it really exists, or coming up with some definition for it, is pretty pointless. Doing that in fact ends up creating more problems than solving them. It's no different debating the existence of an afterlife, or spirits of the dead.

YAMADA: I absolutely agree. Regardless of what's going on in my book, I myself don't believe in the existence of a soul. Like Oshii, I don't care whether it exists or not. If someone thinks it should exist, then that's fine, and anyone who doesn't need one should get by fine without it. It's something like the role which imaginary numbers serve in mathematics. The square root of negative one can play a definite role, but most people never use it in their own personal calculations.

3. DOLLS AND DOGS
Human existence ends up being relative in contrast…

OSHII: What would it mean for a human to "become more than human"? One answer would be to discard the actual human body, and embrace becoming a doll. People try to adjust their natural bodies, evolved for something very different, to the modern urban environment. Instead of following that trajectory, we're better off turning into dolls, into intended artifice.

Another option is to communicate with dogs. Once you discard anthrocentrism, you have to take animals into consideration. Dogs provide a much better contrast against robots or dolls than humans do. Why dogs, though—why not, say, horses, pigs, or turtles? Dogs became unique creatures by interacting and living with humans (cats might stay somewhere in between). You could say that dogs are so close to humans that you have the chance to see furthest into their own depths. By communicating with dogs, I thought humans might realize something about themselves. So I wanted to contrast humans against dogs, rather than simply against artificial intelligences.

YAMADA: I was very conscious of that issue while working on this novel. For me personally, it would be with cats, but I think all you need is the warmth and touch of animals. I imagine being trapped in a building after an earthquake, holding out for rescue. I think having a pet as company would help you hold out emotionally—in fact, I think there would be more consolation than being trapped with fellow humans.

OSHII: When I first began working on *Innocence*, I wasn't conscious of this theme we've been talking about, whether it revolved around dolls or dogs. I only started realizing it, and dealing directly with them, when we actually began to shoot the film. That was the most rewarding part of this whole project. This time I wrote the screenplay, which gave me a lot of the freedom that made such an approach possible. (Oshii's long-time screenwriter Kazunori Ito had penned the original *Ghost in the Shell*, but Oshii took over for *Innocence*. His research for the film included visiting doll museums and companies in the United States, Germany, and Japan. Batou's dog Gabriel is based on Oshii's own beloved basset hound of the same name. Whereas she had made "cameos" in Oshii's films before, in *Innocence* Oshii even brought Gabriel into the recording studio, so that she became the "voice," too, of her own animated version—*ed.*)

4. THE ASTRO BOY FALLACY
How robotic are humans?

YAMADA: Oshii said he wanted to discard anthrocentrism, and I took the same approach. For example, the media always brings up *Astro Boy* whenever it covers robot technology, but I doubt actual robotics engineers have that in mind at all. They just nod to the reporters, because they can't be bothered explaining themselves. I'm no specialist, so I don't know the details, but I think there's a fallacy in the premise of *Astro Boy*, the idea of raising an AI robot like a child in order for it to develop a psyche and an inner life. That could never work. Robots shouldn't be humanized. We're better off pursuing the question off how robotic humans themselves are.

There's no reason why I should believe the people I'm addressing right now are human like me. They might appear to share the same feelings and thoughts I have, because their responses are similar to mine. But they might only be automatons. There's no way to tell they have a psyche. Given that premise, I'd claim that an empty doll is much more innocent than people attached to the illusion of "human-ness." Again, dogs and dolls embody innocence. Humans vacillate, somewhere in between. They aren't even square in a stable middle. Their position is unstable.

OSHII: Exactly. I commute between Mitaka and Kokubunji (in the Western part of Tokyo—*ed.*) on the Chuo line. I ride the train right after school so I see a lot of teenagers. They don't give me the impression of having an interior life. You don't have to be young to appear that way. Middle-aged women and men are no different. They're all just responding to their environment of the train—and I'm sure I look the same to everyone else. I'm not trying to say it's a sign of "contemporary malaise." It's just how humans are.

As Yamada remarked, it's absurd to humanize robots. It would be more relevant to ask what the difference is between an adult raising a child and a girl playing with her doll. It's not an immoral question, nor does it indicate some kind of regression. I just think that's the only way we can understand the nature of human existence.

YAMADA: I read in the paper the other day how scientists realized in the 1990s that the brain contains receptors for the neurohormone oxytocin, which was known to be involved in childbirth, but is now thought to be a major factor in the chemical structure of behaviors like love, trust, and pair-bonding. I don't know how accurate the article was. Discoveries like that change so rapidly.

But it would make sense to me if love could be derived from a chemical process in the brain. In the film *Innocence*, Motoko, who exists now only in cyberspace, has thoughts for Batou, a cyborg. I don't know if those thoughts could be *defined* as love—we do know they are structured as a machine equation. But consider human love as oxytocin—a chemical equation, nine amino acids in a known sequence.

To recognize the parallel is not to denigrate their love, but purify it, make their virtuality congruent with humanity. The rendezvous occurs later in the structure of the film, when Batou heads for his destination by plunging into the ocean, while Motoko descends from the sky. The reason Batou goes into enemy territory isn't really because he wants to rescue someone, nor is it really because he wants to solve the case. He just wants to meet his angel, Motoko. It doesn't really matter whether their relationship is a conventional romance or not. You see, their love might seem cold to humans, but what is between them is no longer human, and now very innocent.

OSHII: If you observe Batou throughout the film, you'll find that his investigation is a formality. He's going through the motions, although for him the motions mean lighting up a yakuza HQ with a squad machine gun and then asking questions of the survivor [*laughter*].

But that's what I wanted. We couldn't possibly have fit everything in a ninety-minute film if we had followed the usual guidelines for narrative. Although this might upset other screenwriters, let me say that when I told the technical director, "There really isn't an investigation," he just laughed. The only clue is the photo of the girl he finds in the book, but that doesn't really tie in nicely with the ending, because the viewer's probably forgotten about it by the time Batou goes on his shooting spree.

Yamada immediately pointed out how Batou has no interest whatsoever in solving a mystery or fighting evil. As far as filmmaking goes, getting the detective story right doesn't matter nearly as much as entertaining the viewer. So the drama ends with Batou meeting Motoko again. And the very final scene depicts the central theme of the entire film: Togusa hugs his daughter, and his daughter holds her doll while Batou is hugging his dog.

5. THAT KIND OF WORLD ONLY HAS GHOSTS
First comes the image that inspires the story.

YAMADA: Whether it's *Beautiful Dreamer*, *Ghost in the Shell*, or *Avalon*, Oshii's films revolve around the theme of disappearance. I think it's a prominent theme in *Innocence* as well. But this time Motoko is "dislocated." I found that very interesting. For example, the empty birdcage in the film obviously signifies the theme of disappearance. When this image is associated with the flying gulls, you realize, ah—that's Motoko.

OSHII: Disappearance and dislocation are almost identical. That kind of world only has ghosts. They wander around a gothic city. Only the animals look upon it in the distance. I immediately came up with this image.

The carnival that Batou and Togusa encounter was based on the annual Dajia Matsu Festival in Taiwan (official English site http://mazu.taichung.gov.tw/English/index.htm—*ed.*). We incorporated many aspects of it, magnifying the scope of the procession, while transplanting it to Etorofu (one of the disputed Kurile Islands north of Japan, developed into an IT research metropolis in the *Ghost in the Shell* future—*ed.*) which we envisioned as a great, Gothic city, as New York. Given a Chinese look, the main avenues become canals. The carnival proceeds down the feet of these buildings like temples. You have no idea what the carnival is for, but it conveys a kind of human presence. The dogs howl sadly and the birds turn above and the flower petals scatter, yet the city sits as still as a stupa.

These images just kept on coming. They were easy for *me* to see, but the actual shooting of them took over a year [*laughter*].

Even with the convenience store scene, I got to fulfill one of my longtime wishes. I wanted to depict a gunfight set in a space crowded with information. I wanted to depict the scattering merchandise as meticulously as possible. In the case of my ideas, it's always the shooting crew that suffers [laughter]. That scene alone required two to three thousand background drawings.

Then I had to figure out how to tie together this disparate collection of scenes. I didn't begin *Innocence* with a story idea. So I'm very interested in seeing how people will respond to the total work. For now, I'm just relieved the film has finally been completed.

ABOUT MASAKI YAMADA

Born in 1950, Masaki Yamada has for three decades been one of the most honored authors in Japanese science fiction, mystery, and adventure fiction. He won the Nihon SF Taisho Award, Japan's equivalent of the Nebula, in 1982 for *The Last Enemy*, and has won the Seiun, the Japanese Hugo, four times, for *Godhunting* (1975), *A Terrestrial Psychohistory* (1978), *The Jewel Thief* (1980), and most recently for his alternate history WWII novel *Kishin Corps* (1995), later adapted into an anime through Geneon Entertainment.

ABOUT MAMORU OSHII

Film director Mamoru Oshii was born in 1951 in Tokyo. He began making independent movies as a college student. In 1977 he was hired by the animation studio Tatsunoko Productions. After leaving Studio Pierrot in 1984, he began to work independently. In the past ten years, Mamoru Oshii has become the anime director whose work has had the greatest influence on world cinema, winning the extensive praise of *Titanic*'s James Cameron and *The Matrix*'s Wachowski brothers. *Ghost in the Shell 2: Innocence* is his seventh anime film. He has also directed five in live-action, including 2000's *Avalon*, shot in Poland and available on U.S. home video through Miramax.